BART SIMPSON BIG SHOT!

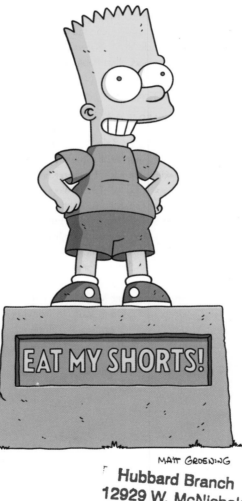

MATT GROENING

HARPER

NEW YORK · LONDON · TORONTO · SYDNEY

BART SIMPSON BIG SHOT!

Collects Bart Simpson Comics 47, 49, 50, 51, 52, and The Simpsons Summer Shindig #1

Copyright © 2013 by
Bongo Entertainment, Inc. All rights reserved.
No part of this book may be used or reproduced in any manner whatsoever
without written permission except in the case of brief quotations
embodied in critical articles and reviews. For information address
HarperCollins Publishers,
195 Broadway, New York, NY 10007.

FIRST EDITION

ISBN 978-0-06-226254-7

16 17 18 19 20 SCP 10 9 8 7 6 5 4 3 2

Publisher: Matt Groening
Creative Director: Nathan Kane
Managing Editor: Terry Delegeane
Director of Operations: Robert Zaugh
Art Director Special Projects: Serban Cristescu
Production Manager: Christopher Ungar
Assistant Art Director: Chia-Hsien Jason Ho
Production/Design: Karen Bates, Nathan Hamill, Art Villanueva
Staff Artist: Mike Rote
Administration: Ruth Waytz, Pete Benson
Editorial Assistant: Max Davison
Legal Guardian: Susan A. Grode

Printed in China

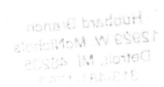

CONTENTS

MAGGIE'S CRIB

by ARAGONÉS

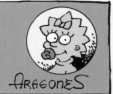

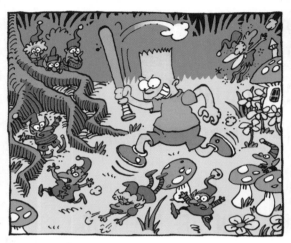

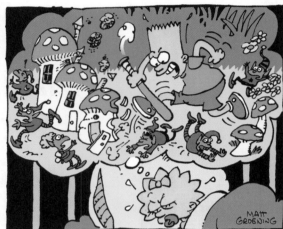

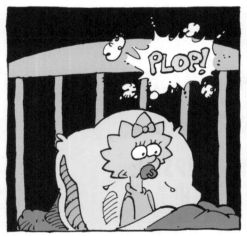

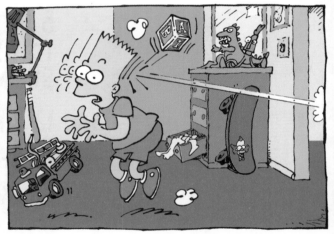

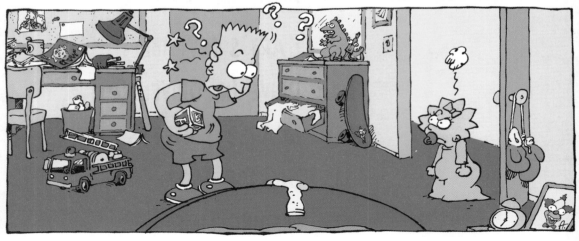

SERGIO ARAGONÉS
STORY & ART

ART VILLANUEVA
COLORS

BILL MORRISON
EDITOR

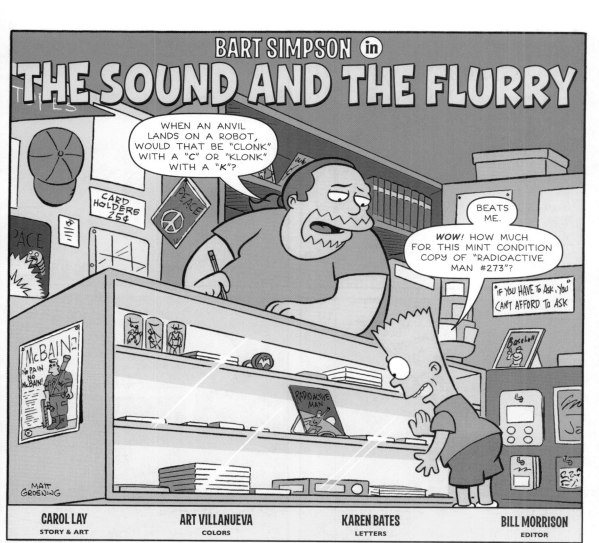

BART SIMPSON in
THE SOUND AND THE FLURRY

WHEN AN ANVIL LANDS ON A ROBOT, WOULD THAT BE "CLONK" WITH A "C" OR "KLONK" WITH A "K"?

BEATS ME.

WOW! HOW MUCH FOR THIS MINT CONDITION COPY OF "RADIOACTIVE MAN #273"?

"IF YOU HAVE TO ASK, YOU CAN'T AFFORD TO ASK"

CAROL LAY
STORY & ART

ART VILLANUEVA
COLORS

KAREN BATES
LETTERS

BILL MORRISON
EDITOR

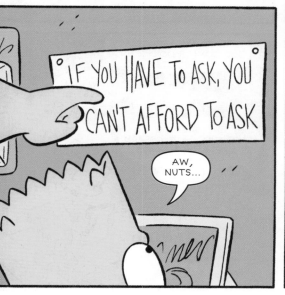

IF YOU HAVE TO ASK, YOU CAN'T AFFORD TO ASK

AW, NUTS...

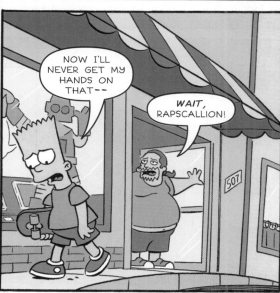

NOW I'LL NEVER GET MY HANDS ON THAT--

WAIT, RAPSCALLION!

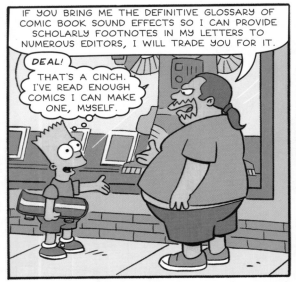

IF YOU BRING ME THE DEFINITIVE GLOSSARY OF COMIC BOOK SOUND EFFECTS SO I CAN PROVIDE SCHOLARLY FOOTNOTES IN MY LETTERS TO NUMEROUS EDITORS, I WILL TRADE YOU FOR IT.

DEAL! THAT'S A CINCH. I'VE READ ENOUGH COMICS I CAN MAKE ONE, MYSELF.

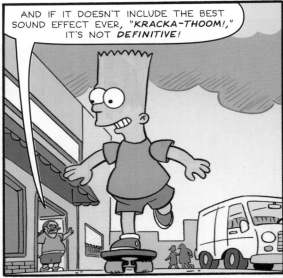

AND IF IT DOESN'T INCLUDE THE BEST SOUND EFFECT EVER, "KRACKA-THOOM!," IT'S NOT DEFINITIVE!

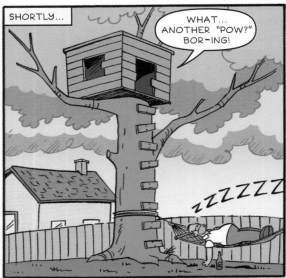

SHORTLY...

WHAT... ANOTHER "POW?" BOR-ING!

ZZZZZZ

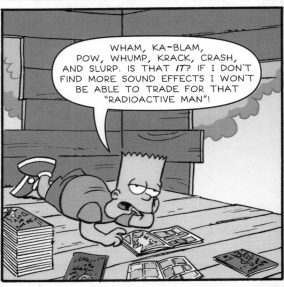

WHAM, KA-BLAM, POW, WHUMP, KRACK, CRASH, AND SLURP. IS THAT IT? IF I DON'T FIND MORE SOUND EFFECTS I WON'T BE ABLE TO TRADE FOR THAT "RADIOACTIVE MAN"!

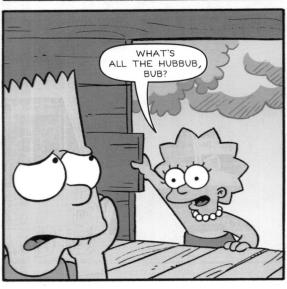

WHAT'S ALL THE HUBBUB, BUB?

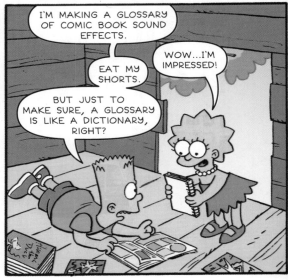

I'M MAKING A GLOSSARY OF COMIC BOOK SOUND EFFECTS.

EAT MY SHORTS.

WOW...I'M IMPRESSED!

BUT JUST TO MAKE SURE, A GLOSSARY IS LIKE A DICTIONARY, RIGHT?

YES. IT'S LIKE A SHORT DICTIONARY FOR SPECIAL SUBJECTS.
DO I NEED MORE THAN 14 WORDS?
POW BLAM
DO YOU WANT IT TO BE *DEFINITIVE*?
THAT WORD SOUNDS FAMILIAR...YEAH.
POW BLAM
RESEARCHING OLD COMICS IS A GOOD START, BUT IT'S LIMITING.
WHAT DO YOU MEAN?
LISTEN. WHAT SOUNDS DO YOU HEAR?
ZZZZZZZ
ZZZZZZ...SNURK... **GNUGHN**...AND FLIB-BIDI-LIBBIDA-BIP.
-LIBBIDA-BIP!
POW BLAM

AND DON'T FORGET PSHHHHHH...
COOL!
ZZZZZZZZ
Snurk!
GNUGHN
FLib-bi
NICE WORK ON THOSE Zs.
SO...YOU THINK I MIGHT BE ANY GOOD AT THIS?
I READ THAT ONE OF THE MOST VALUED CONTRIBUTORS TO THE OXFORD ENGLISH DICTIONARY WAS A MURDERER WHO WAS CONFINED TO A LUNATIC ASYLUM.
I THINK YOU'LL DO ***FINE***.
ZZZZZZZZZZZZ
THANKS, LISA. I JUST GOT AN IDEA FOR SOME ***FIELD RESEARCH***!
Snurk!

HERE GOES NOTHIN'!
TWANG
ZIIIIIP!
SQUAK!!
TOONK!
CLAKITA-CLAKITA-CLAKITA
ZIIIING!
THOOP!
MILK
CREAK
PUMPH!
SPLUT
SLURP
RUMBA
RUMBA
KLONK!
WHA-HUH?!

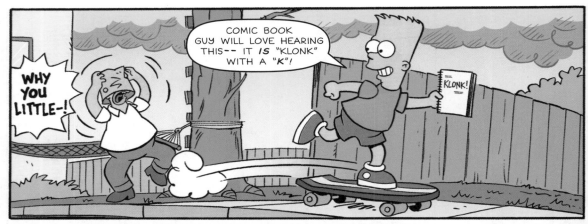

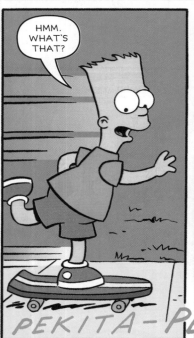

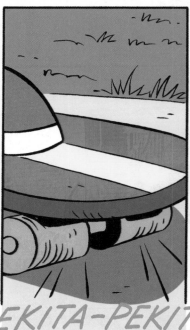

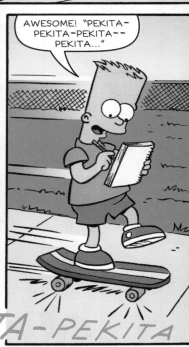

PEKITA-PEKITA-PEKITA-PEKITA

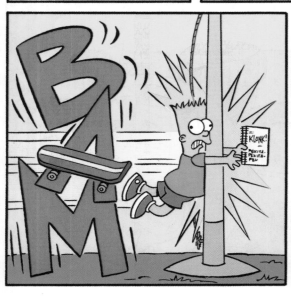

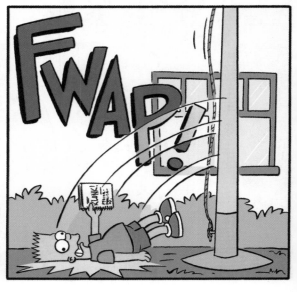

Ohhh...
"FWAP?" COOL!
PUM PUM
PUM PUM PUM PUM
WHAT ARE YOU DOING, DORKUS?
ELEMENTARY SCHOOL
PUM
PUM PUM
FWAP
"PUM PUM PUM: GOON POUNDING FIST INTO HAND."
SMEK!

WAS THAT "SMEK" OR "SMAK"?
HIT ME AGAIN, NELSON.
SMEK!
"SMEK!"
THANKS, NELSON!
OH, MAN. IT'S NO FUN HITTING HIM IF HE LIKES IT...
I'M ALMOST DONE! I JUST NEED TO CONFIRM COMIC BOOK GUY'S FAVORITE SOUND EFFECT, "KRACKA-THOOM!"
TOO BAD NO ONE'S DECLARED WAR ON SPRINGFIELD TODAY.
RUMBLE
RUMBLE

BUT HOLY COW! A BIG BOLT OF LIGHTNING OUGHT TO DO THE TRICK!
AND THIS FLAGPOLE JUST MIGHT GET THAT CLOUD'S ATTENTION!
COME ON, THOR, NORSE GOD OF THUNDER, DO YOUR STUFF!
KRACKA-THOOM!
COMIC BOOK GUY IS RIGHT! IT IS THE BEST SOUND EFFECT OF ALL TIME!

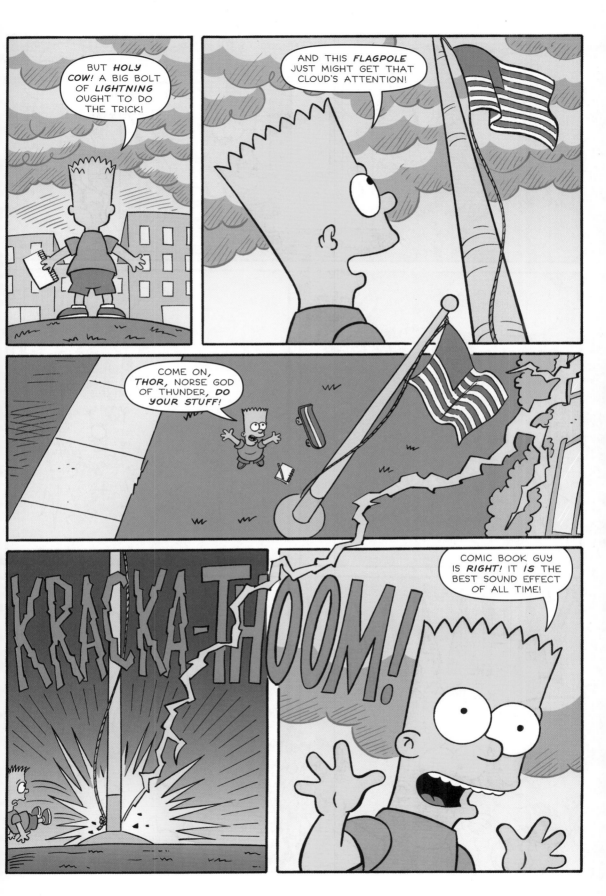

BART! ARE YOU CRAZY!? GET OUT OF THIS THUNDER-STORM!
SILLY SISTER. DON'T YOU KNOW LIGHTNING NEVER STRIKES THE SAME PLACE TWICE?
KRACKA-THOOM!
KRACKA-THOOM!
YAHAAAA!!
KRACKA-THOOM!!
KRACKA-THOOM!!

NOW WHAT AM I GOING TO DO? ALL MY WORK IS JUST A HEAP OF ASHES.
I'LL NEVER GET THAT COPY OF "RADIOACTIVE MAN."
WELL, YOU KNOW WHAT THEY SAY: "IF AT FIRST YOU DON'T SUCCEED..."
C'MON, I'LL HELP YOU. YOU'VE GOT A GOOD START WITH "KRACKA-THOOM!"
KRACKA-THOOM!!
YAAAAAAAAAAAAAA
ZING!
KRACKA-THOOM!!
THE END

Li'l Krusty

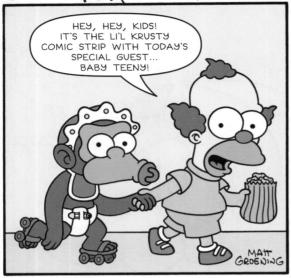

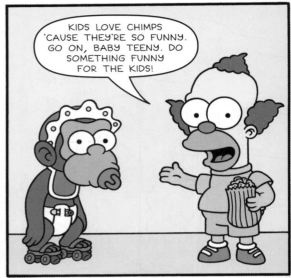

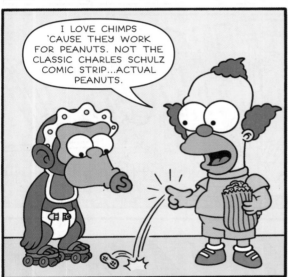

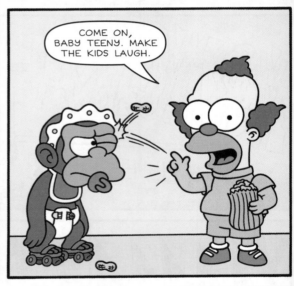

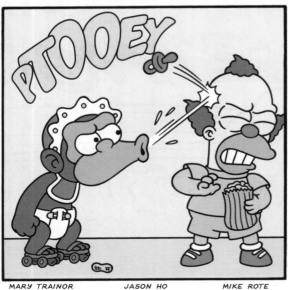

MARY TRAINOR
SCRIPT

JASON HO
PENCILS

MIKE ROTE
INKS

CHRIS UNGAR
COLORS

KAREN BATES
LETTERS

BILL MORRISON
EDITOR

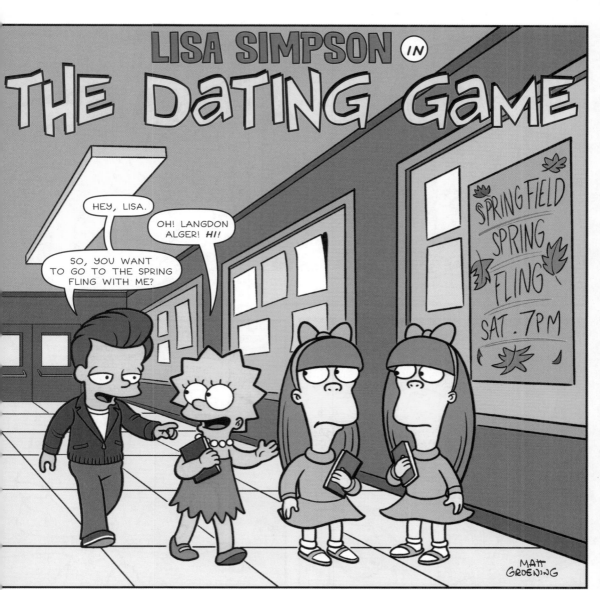

LISA SIMPSON IN
THE DATING GAME

HEY, LISA.

OH! LANGDON ALGER! *HI!*

SO, YOU WANT TO GO TO THE SPRING FLING WITH ME?

SPRINGFIELD SPRING FLING SAT. 7PM

MATT GROENING

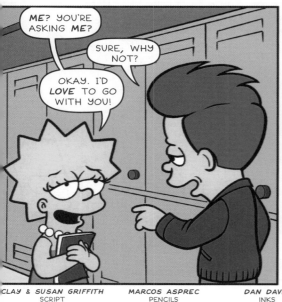

ME? YOU'RE ASKING *ME*?

SURE, WHY NOT?

OKAY. I'D *LOVE* TO GO WITH YOU!

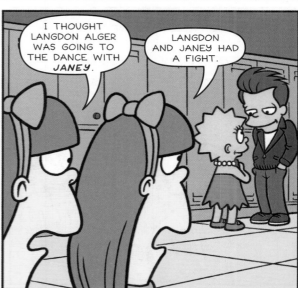

I THOUGHT LANGDON ALGER WAS GOING TO THE DANCE WITH *JANEY*.

LANGDON AND JANEY HAD A FIGHT.

CLAY & SUSAN GRIFFITH
SCRIPT

MARCOS ASPREC
PENCILS

DAN DAVIS
INKS

NATHAN HAMILL
COLORS

KAREN BATES
LETTERS

BILL MORRISON
EDITOR

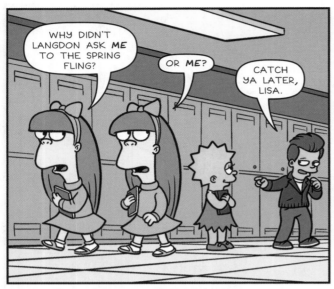

WHY DIDN'T LANGDON ASK *ME* TO THE SPRING FLING?

OR *ME*?

CATCH YA LATER, LISA.

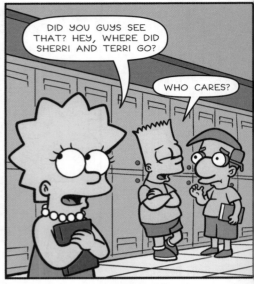

DID YOU GUYS SEE THAT? HEY, WHERE DID SHERRI AND TERRI GO?

WHO CARES?

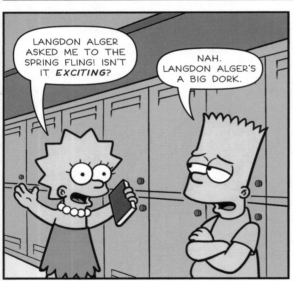

LANGDON ALGER ASKED ME TO THE SPRING FLING! ISN'T IT *EXCITING*?

NAH. LANGDON ALGER'S A BIG DORK.

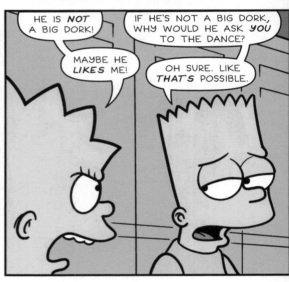

HE IS *NOT* A BIG DORK!

IF HE'S NOT A BIG DORK, WHY WOULD HE ASK *YOU* TO THE DANCE?

MAYBE HE *LIKES* ME!

OH SURE. LIKE *THAT'S* POSSIBLE.

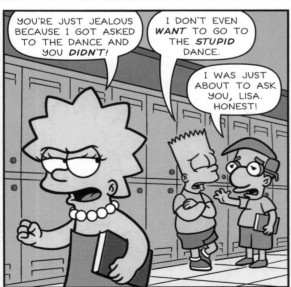

YOU'RE JUST JEALOUS BECAUSE I GOT ASKED TO THE DANCE AND YOU *DIDN'T*!

I DON'T EVEN *WANT* TO GO TO THE *STUPID* DANCE.

I WAS JUST ABOUT TO ASK YOU, LISA. HONEST!

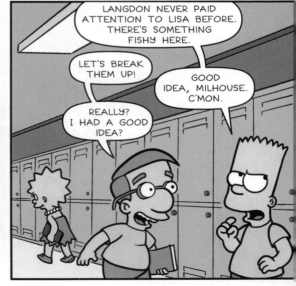

LANGDON NEVER PAID ATTENTION TO LISA BEFORE. THERE'S SOMETHING FISHY HERE.

LET'S BREAK THEM UP!

GOOD IDEA, MILHOUSE. C'MON.

REALLY? I HAD A GOOD IDEA?

SO WHEN LANGDON DUMPS HER, CAN I ASK LISA TO THE DANCE?
SURE...IF YOU WANT TO CATCH A CASE OF ADVANCED COOTIES!
UH...HOW ADVANCED?
AH...AN EMPTY SEAT RIGHT BY MY NEW GIRL, LISA.
UM, LANGDON, HAVE YOU EVER NOTICED THE CEILING IN HERE?
NO REALLY...LOOK. LOOK AT THE CEILING.
BUZZ OFF, MILHOUSE. YOU WEENIE!
SNICKER.
HEH HEH!
OH NO!
CRASH!
LANGDON, I'M SORRY ABOUT BART.
DON'T WORRY ABOUT IT. HE'LL GET HIS. NOW LET ME JUST--

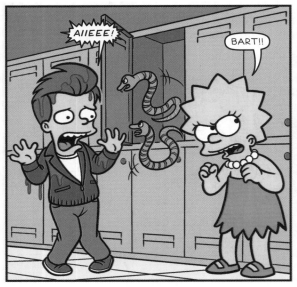

AIIEEE!

BART!!

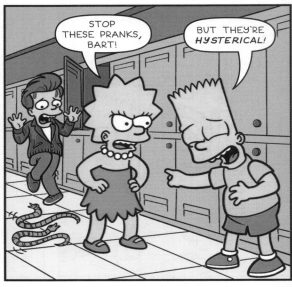

STOP THESE PRANKS, BART!

BUT THEY'RE *HYSTERICAL!*

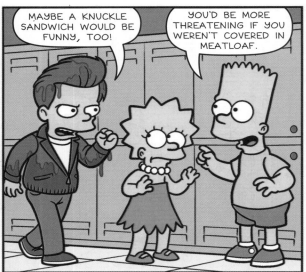

MAYBE A KNUCKLE SANDWICH WOULD BE FUNNY, TOO!

YOU'D BE MORE THREATENING IF YOU WEREN'T COVERED IN MEATLOAF.

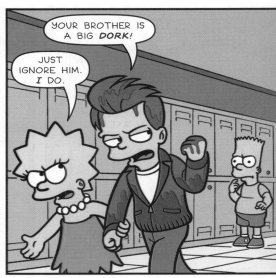

YOUR BROTHER IS A BIG *DORK!*

JUST IGNORE HIM. *I* DO.

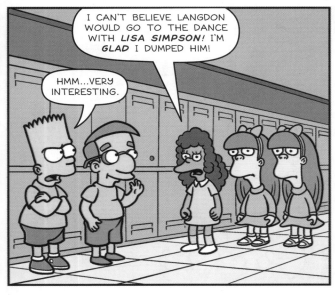

I CAN'T BELIEVE LANGDON WOULD GO TO THE DANCE WITH *LISA SIMPSON!* I'M *GLAD* I DUMPED HIM!

HMM...VERY INTERESTING.

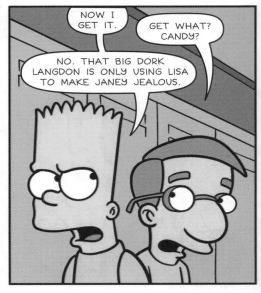

NOW I GET IT.

GET WHAT? CANDY?

NO. THAT BIG DORK LANGDON IS ONLY USING LISA TO MAKE JANEY JEALOUS.

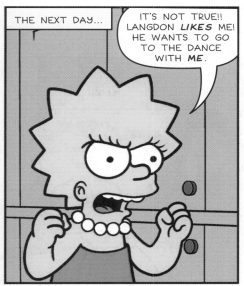

THE NEXT DAY...

IT'S NOT TRUE!! LANGDON *LIKES* ME! HE WANTS TO GO TO THE DANCE WITH *ME*.

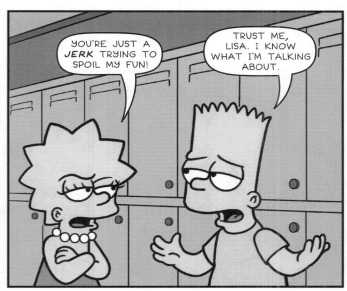

YOU'RE JUST A *JERK* TRYING TO SPOIL MY FUN!

TRUST ME, LISA. I KNOW WHAT I'M TALKING ABOUT.

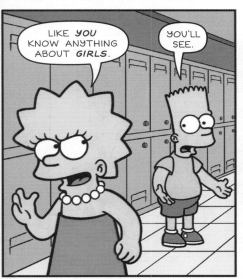

LIKE *YOU* KNOW ANYTHING ABOUT *GIRLS*.

YOU'LL SEE.

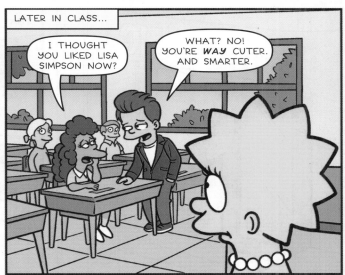

LATER IN CLASS...

I THOUGHT YOU LIKED LISA SIMPSON NOW?

WHAT? NO! YOU'RE *WAY* CUTER. AND SMARTER.

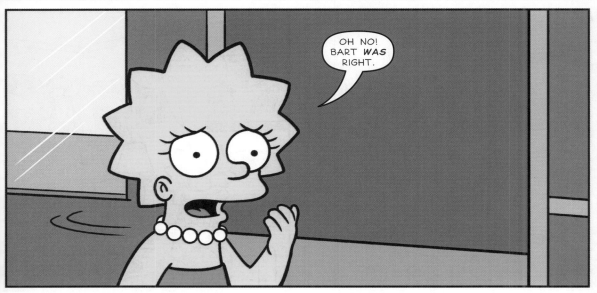

OH NO! BART *WAS* RIGHT.

I *WON'T* BE GOING TO THE DANCE WITH YOU, LANGDON.
OH... OKAY.
SO, JANEY... WANT TO GO TO THE SPRING FLING?
YES! OH, LANGDON! I THOUGHT YOU'D NEVER ASK!
SPRING FLING
I DIDN'T EVEN WANT TO WEAR A *FANCY* DRESS AND GO TO THAT *STUPID* DANCE ANYWAY.
THAT SATURDAY NIGHT...
WHAT ARE YOU LOOKING AT, YOU SILLY DRESS?
JAZZ FEST
OH, LISA! YOU'LL LOOK SO BEAUTIFUL IN ME AT THE SPRING FLING!
WELL FORGET IT! I'M *NOT* GOING!

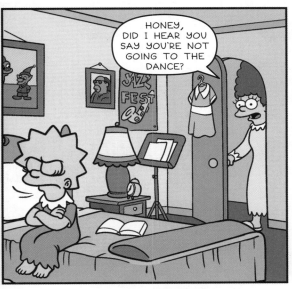

HONEY, DID I HEAR YOU SAY YOU'RE NOT GOING TO THE DANCE?

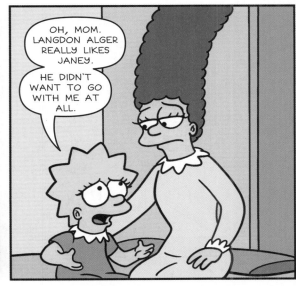

OH, MOM. LANGDON ALGER REALLY LIKES JANEY.

HE DIDN'T WANT TO GO WITH ME AT ALL.

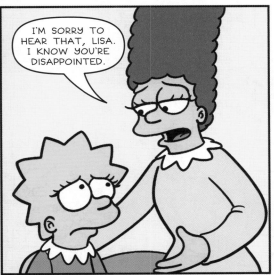

I'M SORRY TO HEAR THAT, LISA. I KNOW YOU'RE DISAPPOINTED.

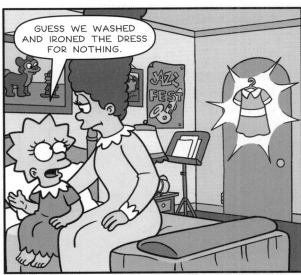

GUESS WE WASHED AND IRONED THE DRESS FOR NOTHING.

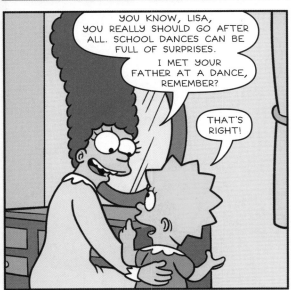

YOU KNOW, LISA, YOU REALLY SHOULD GO AFTER ALL. SCHOOL DANCES CAN BE FULL OF SURPRISES.

I MET YOUR FATHER AT A DANCE, REMEMBER?

THAT'S RIGHT!

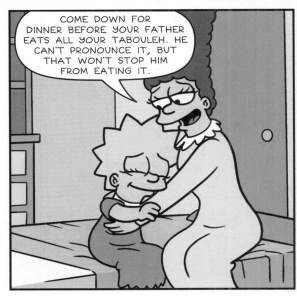

COME DOWN FOR DINNER BEFORE YOUR FATHER EATS ALL YOUR TABOULEH. HE CAN'T PRONOUNCE IT, BUT THAT WON'T STOP HIM FROM EATING IT.

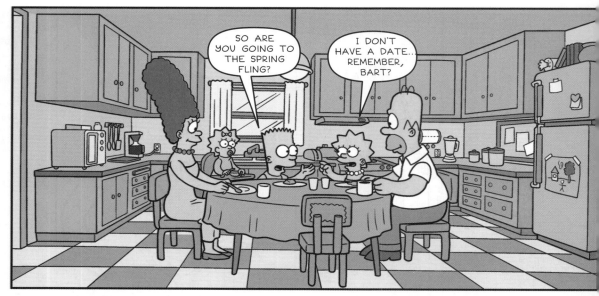

SO ARE YOU GOING TO THE SPRING FLING?

I DON'T HAVE A DATE... REMEMBER, BART?

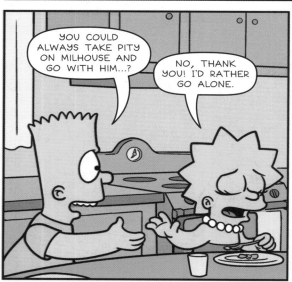

YOU COULD ALWAYS TAKE PITY ON MILHOUSE AND GO WITH HIM...?

NO, THANK YOU! I'D RATHER GO ALONE.

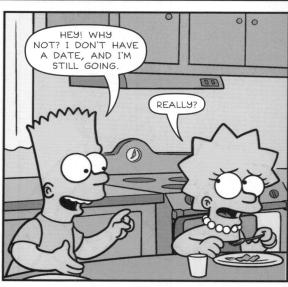

HEY! WHY NOT? I DON'T HAVE A DATE, AND I'M STILL GOING.

REALLY?

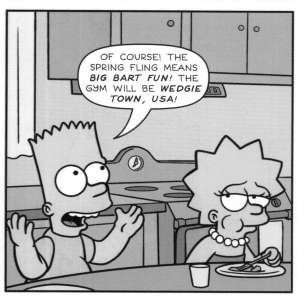

OF COURSE! THE SPRING FLING MEANS *BIG BART FUN!* THE GYM WILL BE *WEDGIE TOWN, USA!*

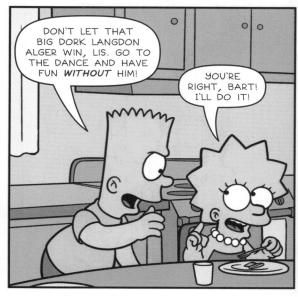

DON'T LET THAT BIG DORK LANGDON ALGER WIN, LIS. GO TO THE DANCE AND HAVE FUN *WITHOUT* HIM!

YOU'RE RIGHT, BART! I'LL DO IT!

SPRING FLING
HAVE FUN YOU TWO.
BART! GIVE ME THE KETCHUP PACKETS AND THE WATER BALLOONS.
AW, MAN...
OH, WHAT AM I DOING HERE?
I SHOULDN'T HAVE COME! I DON'T WANT ANYONE TO SEE ME.
I'LL LOOK PATHETIC.
SPRING FLING
AW, MAN...I CAN'T BELIEVE THIS!
DUDE, WHAT ARE WE GONNA DO?
WHAT'S THE MATTER?
WE'RE WITH THE BAND. BUT OUR SAXOPHONE PLAYER IS A NO-SHOW!
YEAH, LIKE, HIS PARENTS TOTALLY GROUNDED HIM.

CAN I HELP?
ONLY IF YOU CAN BLOW A SAX, LITTLE LADY.
FUNNY YOU SHOULD MENTION IT...
SPRING FLING
THIS BAND IS GREAT!
THE SAX PLAYER IS FANTASTIC!
THAT'S NOT JUST ANY SAX PLAYER...THAT'S *LISA SIMPSON!*
WAY TO WAIL, LISA!
YEAH! ARE YOU AVAILABLE FOR OUR NEXT GIG?
LISA IS SO COOL!
YEAH... SHE'S SOMETHING **SPECIAL** ALL RIGHT!!
WAY TO GO, LISA.
SPLOOSH!
YOU BIG DORK!
THE END

Li'L KRUSTY

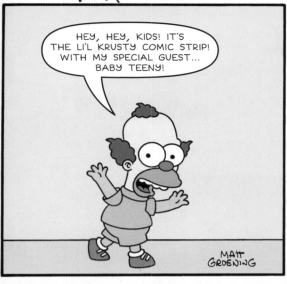

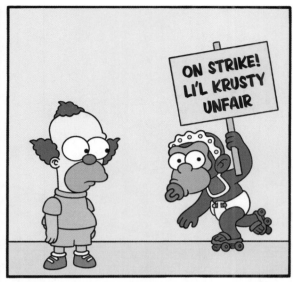

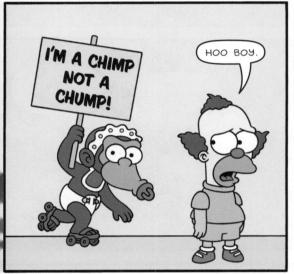

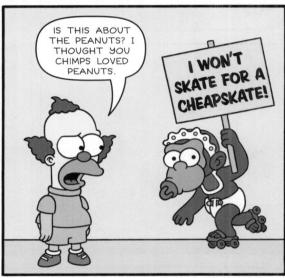

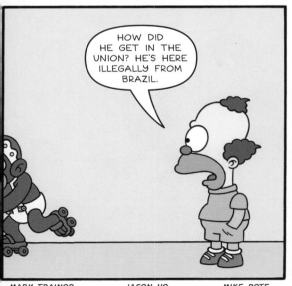

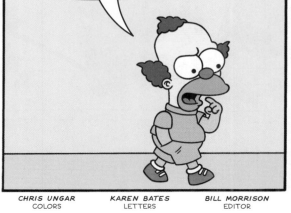

MARY TRAINOR
SCRIPT

JASON HO
PENCILS

MIKE ROTE
INKS

CHRIS UNGAR
COLORS

KAREN BATES
LETTERS

BILL MORRISON
EDITOR

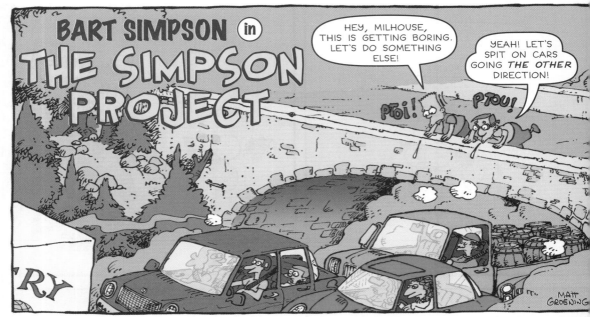

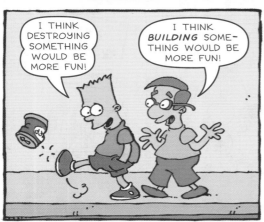

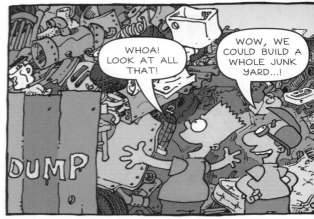

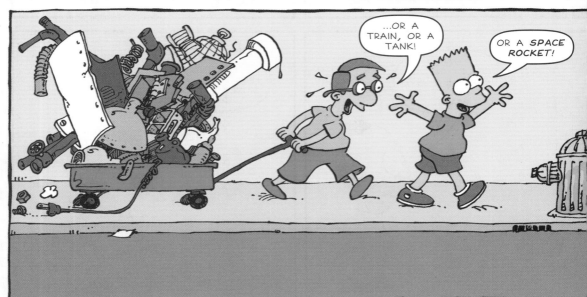

SERGIO ARAGONÉS
SCRIPT & ART

ART VILLANUEVA
COLORS

KAREN BATES
LETTERS

BILL MORRISON
EDITOR

YOUR DAD'S TOOLS SURE CAME IN HANDY!
YOU MEAN **MR. FLANDERS'** TOOLS?
WHAT'S ALL THAT RACKET? WHAT ARE THOSE BOYS DOING IN THE FRONT YARD?
THEY'RE MAKING A MESS OF THE LAWN!
I'LL TELL THEM TO GO SOMEPLACE ELSE!
LET THEM STAY, MOM. OTHERWISE THEY'LL JUST CREATE HAVOC SOMEPLACE ELSE.
HRRMMM...
WHAT HARM CAN THEY DO?
DON'T YOU NEED PERMISSION FROM YOUR DAD TO USE THAT?
NAH. I USE IT MORE THAN **HE** DOES!
PRAUW..
PRAW!.

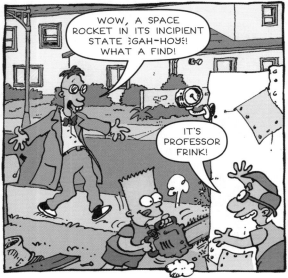

WOW, A SPACE ROCKET IN ITS INCIPIENT STATE ¿GAH-HOY?! WHAT A FIND!

IT'S PROFESSOR FRINK!

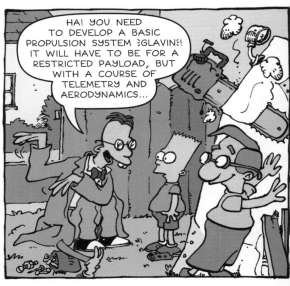

HA! YOU NEED TO DEVELOP A BASIC PROPULSION SYSTEM ¿GLAVIN?! IT WILL HAVE TO BE FOR A RESTRICTED PAYLOAD, BUT WITH A COURSE OF TELEMETRY AND AERODYNAMICS...

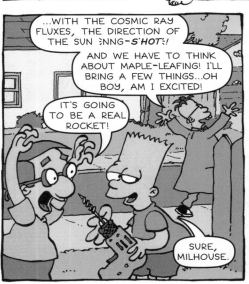

...WITH THE COSMIC RAY FLUXES, THE DIRECTION OF THE SUN ¿NNG-S'HOT?!

AND WE HAVE TO THINK ABOUT MAPLE-LEAFING! I'LL BRING A FEW THINGS...OH BOY, AM I EXCITED!

IT'S GOING TO BE A REAL ROCKET!

SURE, MILHOUSE.

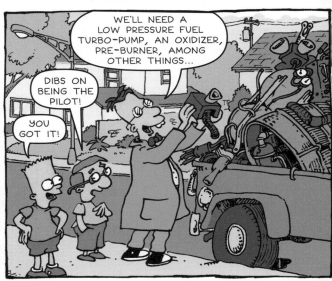

WE'LL NEED A LOW PRESSURE FUEL TURBO-PUMP, AN OXIDIZER, PRE-BURNER, AMONG OTHER THINGS...

DIBS ON BEING THE PILOT!

YOU GOT IT!

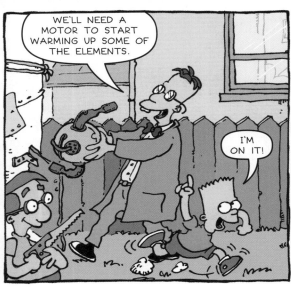

WE'LL NEED A MOTOR TO START WARMING UP SOME OF THE ELEMENTS.

I'M ON IT!

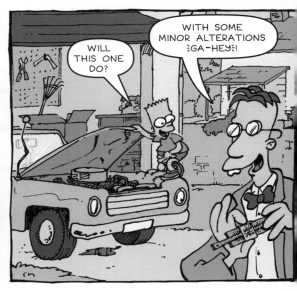

WILL THIS ONE DO?

WITH SOME MINOR ALTERATIONS ¿GA-HEY?!

30

THANKS FOR THE LADDER, MR. FLANDERS!
OKILY-DOKILY, MILHOUSE!
HERE YOU ARE, BART. HIC! ANYTHING FOR SCIENCE!
TO THE MOO
OIL
SIMPSON
WHO SAYS NOTHING HAPPENS IN SPRINGFIELD? THEY'RE BUILDING A ***ROCKET***!
CHAN 4 NEWS
SO, TELL US ALL ABOUT IT, PROFESSOR FRINK!
SCIENCE CANNOT BE DETERRED! FIRST, THE MOON, AND NOW, WITH THIS YOUNGSTER'S AMBITIONS... WELL, MAYBE ***MARS***, WOULDN'T THAT BE EXCITING!
YOU HEARD IT RIGHT HERE, SPRINGFIELD'S FIRST INDEPENDENT MANNED FLIGHT TO MARS!
HISTORY NASA
SKYLAB
NASA
SPACE
STAR WARS
SPACE TECHNOLOGY
I'VE TOLD YOU, INDEPENDENT CONTRACTORS ARE PROLIFERATING! INDIA, BRAZIL, PAKISTAN, AND NOW, ***SPRINGFIELD***!
NASA
WHERE IS SPRINGFIELD?

THEY'RE BUILDING THE ROCKET AT THE RESIDENCE OF HOMER SIMPSON, AN EMPLOYEE OF THE SPRINGFIELD NUCLEAR POWER PLANT!
THEY HAVE ACCESS TO NUCLEAR POWER!
THAT PLANT IS STRICTLY TO BE USED FOR PROVIDING THE COMMUNITY WITH ELECTRICITY!
I'LL CALL THE OWNER!
NASA
AHOY-HOY! YES, THIS IS HE!
WHAT...? NASA...? I SHOULDN'T WHAT...? FOR WHAT...?
NOBODY TELLS CHARLES MONTGOMERY BURNS WHAT TO DO!!
THE NERVE OF SOME OUTSIDERS... SMITHERS!
SEND EVERY-THING THAT'S NECESSARY FOR A SPACE LAUNCH OVER TO THE SIMPSON'S RESIDENCE!
ARE YOU SURE, SIR?
C.M. BURNS
HMM... NASA...WHAT IS NASA...?
I'D BETTER DO IT! THAT CALL WAS FROM NASA!

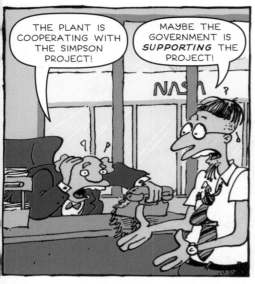

THE PLANT IS COOPERATING WITH THE SIMPSON PROJECT!

MAYBE THE GOVERNMENT IS *SUPPORTING* THE PROJECT!

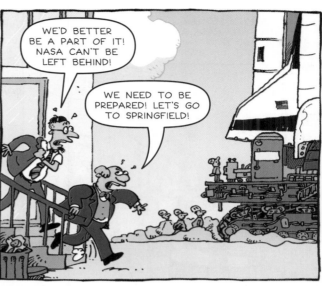

WE'D BETTER BE A PART OF IT! NASA CAN'T BE LEFT BEHIND!

WE NEED TO BE PREPARED! LET'S GO TO SPRINGFIELD!

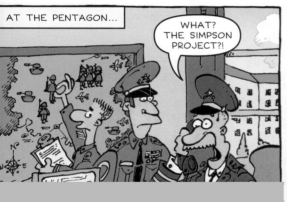

AT THE PENTAGON...

WHAT? THE SIMPSON PROJECT?!

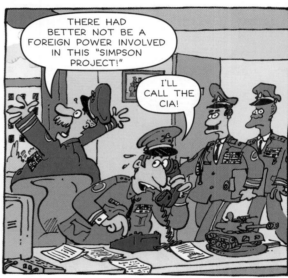

THERE HAD BETTER NOT BE A FOREIGN POWER INVOLVED IN THIS "SIMPSON PROJECT!"

I'LL CALL THE CIA!

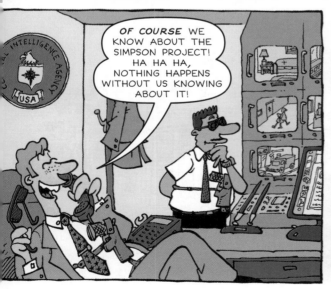

OF COURSE WE KNOW ABOUT THE SIMPSON PROJECT! HA HA HA, NOTHING HAPPENS WITHOUT US KNOWING ABOUT IT!

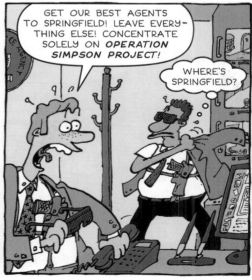

GET OUR BEST AGENTS TO SPRINGFIELD! LEAVE EVERYTHING ELSE! CONCENTRATE SOLELY ON *OPERATION SIMPSON PROJECT!*

WHERE'S SPRINGFIELD?

SPRINGFIELD NUCLEAR PLANT AND NASA ARE WITH THEM, AND NOW THE MILITARY IS GETTING INVOLVED!
WE'D BETTER TELL THE PRESIDENT!
COMRADE! I JUST HAVE INTERCEPTED ULTRA-SECRET MESSAGE FROM CIA!
KGB
VODKA
COMRADES...THEY ARE BUILDING ANOTHER MILITARY LAUNCHING PAD IN SECRET LOCATION CALLED SPRINGFIELD!
YES, GET OUR AGENTS OVER THERE...NO, I DON'T KNOW IN WHICH STATE IS SPRINGFIELD LOCATED! IS A SECRET! YOU FIND IT!
IS FRANCE OR ISRAEL INVOLVED?
MAYBE CHINA IS IN ON IT! LET'S CALL THE CHAIRMAN!!
YES, MR. PRESIDENT, IT'S CONFIRMED BY THE PENTAGON, NASA, THE CIA... AND WE THINK OTHER COUNTRIES KNOW ABOUT IT, TOO!
MULCH

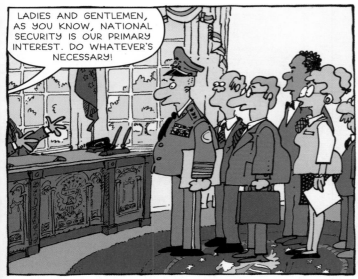

LADIES AND GENTLEMEN, AS YOU KNOW, NATIONAL SECURITY IS OUR PRIMARY INTEREST. DO WHATEVER'S NECESSARY!

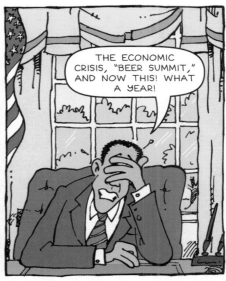

THE ECONOMIC CRISIS, "BEER SUMMIT," AND NOW THIS! WHAT A YEAR!

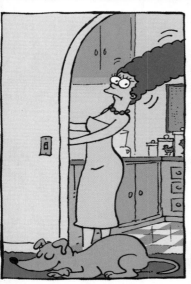

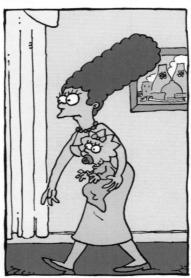

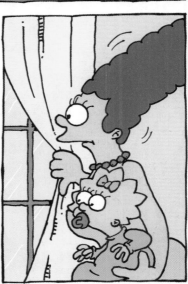

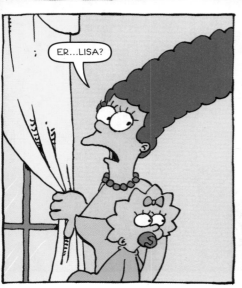

ER...LISA?

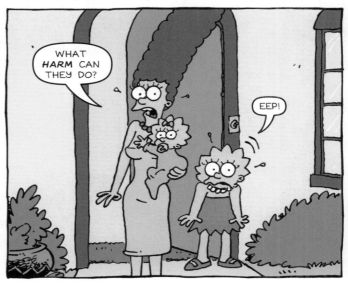

WHAT *HARM* CAN THEY DO?

EEP!

UNITED STATES ARMY
609
SWAT
AS YOU CAN SEE, WITH A FEW MODIFICATIONS, WE CAN REALLY ⁝FLA-HOYBEN⁝ GO PLACES!
HEY, ALL OF YOU, PAY ATTENTION! I HAVE JURISDICTION!
TO THE MOON
IT'S THE APOCALYPSE! "VERILY I SAY UNTO YOU, ALL THESE THINGS SHALL COME UPON THIS GENERATION." IT'S IN ***REVELATION!***
I THINK I FOUND THE NUT THAT CAUSED ALL THIS!
MOVE IT! WE NEED THE SPACE FOR THE FORTY OTHER TRUCKS!

YOU HEARD IT HERE FIRST. SPRINGFIELD HAS NOW JOINED NASA AS ONE OF THE MOST IMPORTANT PLAYERS IN THE INTERNATIONAL FIELD OF ASTRONAUTICS!
AND NOW, WE'LL INTERVIEW THE FIRST WOMAN EVER TO TAKE A TRIP TO MARS!
SURE, I SEE ⁝HIC!⁝ WHAT'S WRONG WITH THIS PICTURE! MY MOTOR IS MISSING! HEE HEE...
RIGHT...⁝HIC!⁝ AND I KNOW WHERE IT WENT...I THINK. ⁝BRRAPPP!⁝
DANGER
SPRINGFIELD NUCLEAR PLANT
DANGER
SPRINGFIELD NUCLEAR PLANT
SIMPSON
US ARMY
US ARMY
SPRINGFIELD 6 CHANNEL NEWS
NASA
FLOWERS BY IRENE
OF COURSE THE MILITARY IS INVOLVED! THEY ARE PROTECTING THE SITE!
YES, THE RUSSIANS ARE IN ON IT! I HAVE THEIR REPRESENTATIVE HERE NEXT TO ME!
ARAGONES 09

THIS...THIS THING IS A TOY!
IS THIS A HOAX?
A HOAX?
OF COURSE IT'S A HOAX! ISN'T IT OBVIOUS?
WE KNEW IT ALL THE TIME!
YOU TELL THE PRESIDENT!
NO, YOU TELL THE PRESIDENT!
BUT...BUT I WAS JUST HELPING THE KIDS!
YEAH, TELL IT TO THE CHIEF!
WAIT A MINUTE, I AM THE CHIEF!
WHERE IS BART?
YEAH, WHERE IS BART?
WASN'T I RIGHT, MILHOUSE? THIS IS MORE FUN THAN BUILDING ANYTHING!
PTOU!
YOU'RE RIGHT, BART! I DON'T THINK WE MISSED ANYTHING BY NOT STAYING TO HELP PROFESSOR FRINK!
END

LI'L KRUSTY

WELL, KIDS, APPARENTLY BABY TEENY DOESN'T WORK FOR PEANUTS. WE SETTLED ON A PAYMENT OF ONE BANANA PER APPEARANCE.
MATT GROENING
SO NOW, BABY TEENY, I'M GONNA TEACH YOU THE BASICS OF A SIX-PANEL COMIC STRIP. JUST KEEP IN MIND, IT'S ALL ABOUT ENDING WITH A BIG LAUGH.
WE INTRODUCE THE CHARACTERS UP THERE IN THE FIRST TWO PANELS, SEE?
THE SET UP GOES HERE, IN THE FOURTH PANEL. MAYBE WE GIVE IT SOME FORESHADOWING...YOU KNOW, AN INDICATION OF WHAT'S ABOUT TO HAPPEN...
...THEN THE GAG GOES HERE IN THE FIFTH--
YIIIIIIIIII!!!!
I MEAN IT, KIDS...IF ANYBODY LAUGHS, I'M CANCELLING THIS COMIC STRIP!

MARY TRAINOR SCRIPT
JASON HO PENCILS
MIKE ROTE INKS
CHRIS UNGAR COLORS
KAREN BATES LETTERS
BILL MORRISON EDITOR

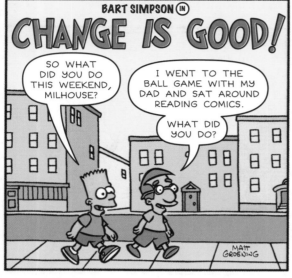

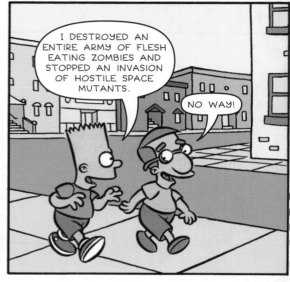

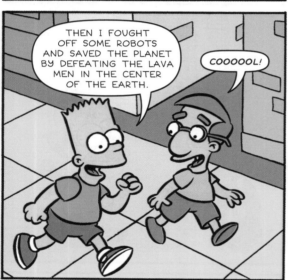

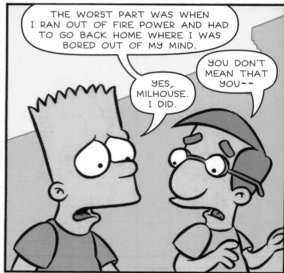

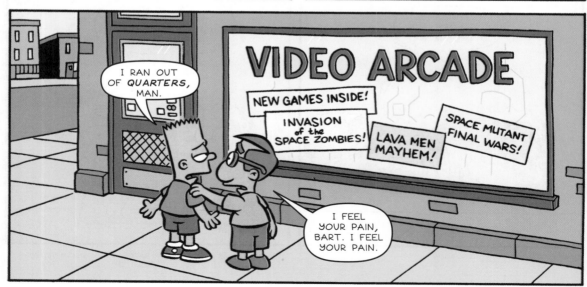

CHRIS YAMBAR
SCRIPT

MIKE KAZALEH
PENCILS & INKS

ART VILLANUEVA
COLORS

KAREN BATES
LETTERS

BILL MORRISON
EDITOR

CHILDREN OFF THE COB

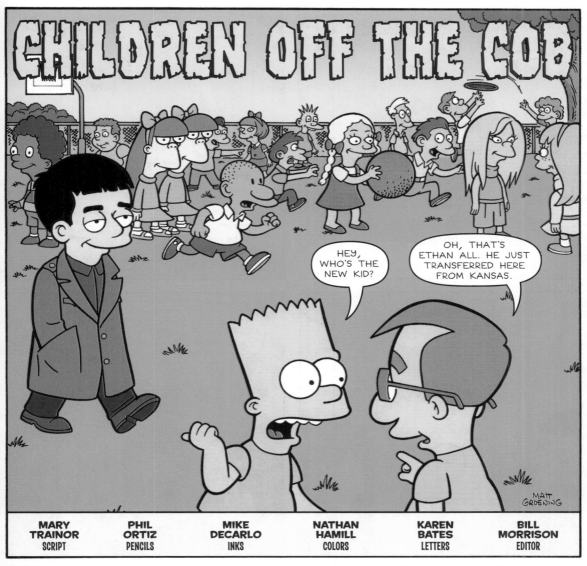

HEY, WHO'S THE NEW KID?

OH, THAT'S ETHAN ALL. HE JUST TRANSFERRED HERE FROM KANSAS.

MATT GROENING

| **MARY TRAINOR** SCRIPT | **PHIL ORTIZ** PENCILS | **MIKE DECARLO** INKS | **NATHAN HAMILL** COLORS | **KAREN BATES** LETTERS | **BILL MORRISON** EDITOR |

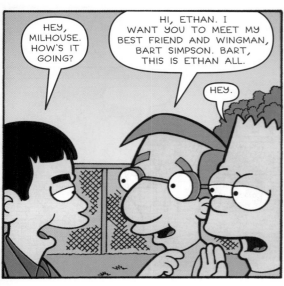

HEY, MILHOUSE. HOW'S IT GOING?

HI, ETHAN. I WANT YOU TO MEET MY BEST FRIEND AND WINGMAN, BART SIMPSON. BART, THIS IS ETHAN ALL.

HEY.

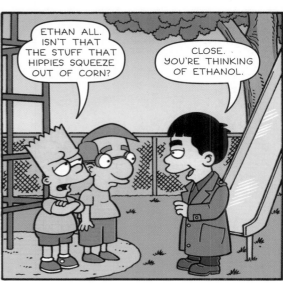

ETHAN ALL. ISN'T THAT THE STUFF THAT HIPPIES SQUEEZE OUT OF CORN?

CLOSE. YOU'RE THINKING OF ETHANOL.

SO WHAT DO KIDS DO FOR FUN IN KANSAS?
WE GROW CORN.
OOOOH... SOUNDS REAL CUTTING EDGE, DUDE.
ACTUALLY IT IS, BART. DID YOU KNOW THAT CORN IS THE CLEANEST, GREENEST SOURCE OF RENEWABLE FUEL?
WHOA, GREEN ENERGY. I LIKE THAT!
AND DID YOU KNOW THAT WITH THE GREAT DEMAND FOR ALTERNATIVE FUEL, PLANTING CORN IS LIKE PLANTING MONEY TREES.
WHOA. GREENBACKS, *I* LIKE ***THAT!***
SOON, HAVING A CORNFIELD WILL BE THE NEW STATUS SYMBOL. EVERYONE WILL BE WISHING THEY HAD ONE OF THEIR OWN!
WHOA, GREEN WITH ENVY. *I* LIKE ***THAT!***
IT'S TRUE! IN THE PAST FEW YEARS, DOMESTIC PRODUCTION OF ETHANOL FROM CORN HAS MORE THAN DOUBLED!
WHOA, DOUBLED! ***WE*** LIKE ***THAT!***
THAT'S RIGHT, ETHANOL PRODUCTION IS SKYROCKETING! HAVING A CORNFIELD IS LIKE HAVING AN ATM MACHINE IN YOUR BACKYARD!
KA-CHING!

BOYS AND GIRLS OF SPRINGFIELD, I'M HERE TO TELL YOU THAT CORN IS THE FUTURE! CORN IS KING!
LONG LIVE CORN!
CORN RULES!
CORN KICKS BUTT!
ETHAN ALL! ETHANOL! ALL FOR ONE AND ONE FOR ALL!
COUNT ME IN!
UND ME, ALSO!
WHERE DO I SIGN UP?
HERE'S A PACKET OF CORN SEEDS FOR EACH OF YOU TO START WITH. SOW THE SEEDS HALF AN INCH TO AN INCH DEEP, FOUR TO SIX INCHES APART.
BE SURE THE PLANTS GET AT LEAST AN INCH OF WATER A WEEK...
...AND, MOST IMPORTANTLY OF ALL, MAKE SURE YOU GIVE THE CORN YOUR COMPLETE AND UTTER DEVOTION!

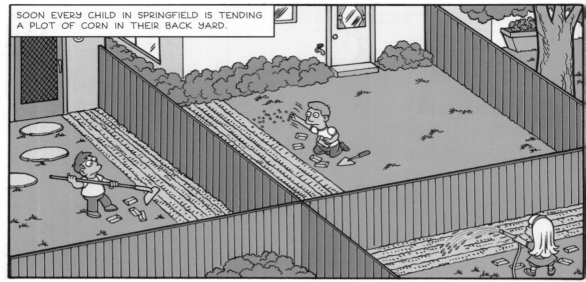

SOON EVERY CHILD IN SPRINGFIELD IS TENDING A PLOT OF CORN IN THEIR BACK YARD.

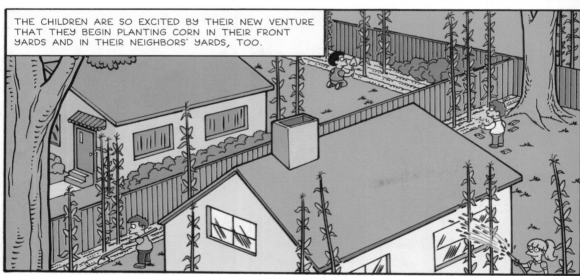

THE CHILDREN ARE SO EXCITED BY THEIR NEW VENTURE THAT THEY BEGIN PLANTING CORN IN THEIR FRONT YARDS AND IN THEIR NEIGHBORS' YARDS, TOO.

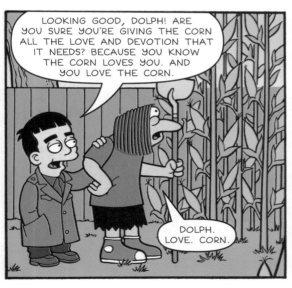

LOOKING GOOD, DOLPH! ARE YOU SURE YOU'RE GIVING THE CORN ALL THE LOVE AND DEVOTION THAT IT NEEDS? BECAUSE YOU KNOW THE CORN LOVES YOU. AND YOU LOVE THE CORN.

DOLPH. LOVE. CORN.

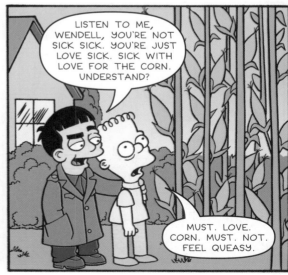

LISTEN TO ME, WENDELL, YOU'RE NOT SICK SICK. YOU'RE JUST LOVE SICK. SICK WITH LOVE FOR THE CORN. UNDERSTAND?

MUST. LOVE. CORN. MUST. NOT. FEEL QUEASY.

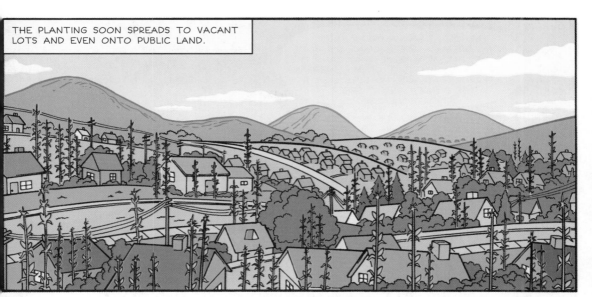

THE PLANTING SOON SPREADS TO VACANT LOTS AND EVEN ONTO PUBLIC LAND.

BEFORE LONG, STALKS OF CORN GROW IN EVERY SQUARE FOOT OF OPEN SPACE IN SPRINGFIELD

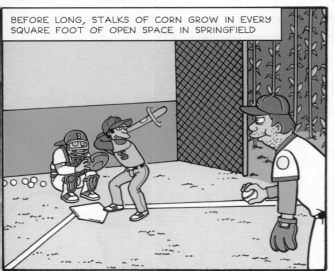

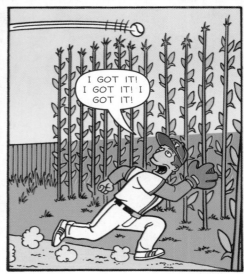

I GOT IT! I GOT IT! I GOT IT!

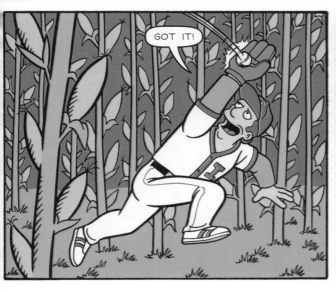

GOT IT!

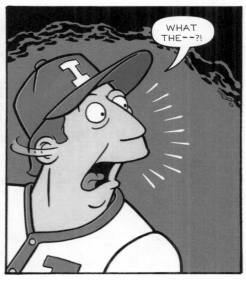

WHAT THE--?!

BEHOLD! I HAD A DREAM, AND IN MY DREAM A GREEN GIANT DID COME TO ME, AND IT WAS HE WHO CANS THE CORN, AND I DID FALL ON MY KNEES IN TERROR, AND HIDE MY EYES LEST I BE BLINDED BY HIS SHEER AWESOMENESS!
AND THEN HE WHO CANS THE CORN TOLD ME THE CORN SHALL INHERIT THE EARTH! THIS IS HIS WILL AND WE MUST OBEY!
MUST. OBEY. CORN.

OUTFIELDER! OUTFIELDER! CAST HIM OUT OF THE CORNFIELD!
THUNK

OUTFIELDER! OUTFIELDER!

IS IT JUST ME OR ARE THINGS STARTING TO GET CREEPY AROUND HERE?
OH, WE'VE DEFINITELY CROSSED A LINE.
UH...ETHAN. CAN'T HELP BUT NOTICE THAT YOU'VE TAKING THIS WHOLE CORN THING IN A REALLY WEIRD DIRECTION...
A-HA! HE WHO CANS THE CORN SO PROPHESIED THAT UNBELIEVERS SHALL APPEAR AMONGST US. AND THESE UNBELIEVERS WILL PROFANE THE CORN.
OKAY. THAT'S IT. I'M OUT OF HERE, DUDE.
I'M RIGHT BEHIND YOU, BROTHER!
STOP THEM! DISOBEDIENCE TO ME IS DISOBEDIENCE TO HE WHO CANS THE CORN!
PUT THE UNBELIEVERS IN THE CORN SILO! THEY WILL DROWN IN THE SWEET KERNELS OF OUR FIRST HARVEST.
MUST. OBEY. CORN.
ETHAN ALL! ETHANOL! I TOLD YOU NO ONE NAMES THEIR KID AFTER CORN JUICE!

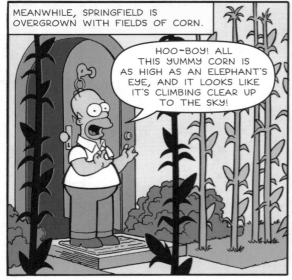

MEANWHILE, SPRINGFIELD IS OVERGROWN WITH FIELDS OF CORN.

HOO-BOY! ALL THIS YUMMY CORN IS AS HIGH AS AN ELEPHANT'S EYE, AND IT LOOKS LIKE IT'S CLIMBING CLEAR UP TO THE SKY!

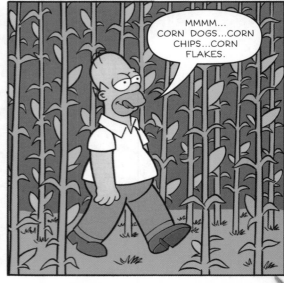

MMMM... CORN DOGS...CORN CHIPS...CORN FLAKES.

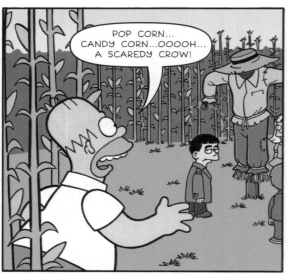

POP CORN... CANDY CORN...OOOOH... A SCAREDY CROW!

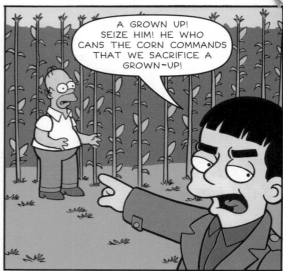

A GROWN UP! SEIZE HIM! HE WHO CANS THE CORN COMMANDS THAT WE SACRIFICE A GROWN-UP!

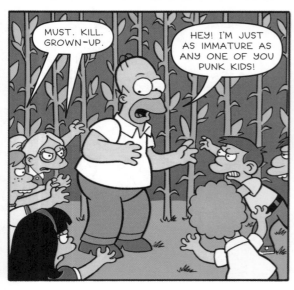

MUST. KILL. GROWN-UP.

HEY! I'M JUST AS IMMATURE AS ANY ONE OF YOU PUNK KIDS!

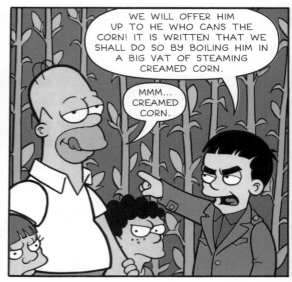

WE WILL OFFER HIM UP TO HE WHO CANS THE CORN! IT IS WRITTEN THAT WE SHALL DO SO BY BOILING HIM IN A BIG VAT OF STEAMING CREAMED CORN.

MMM... CREAMED CORN.

YOU KNOW, KIDS, MARGE ALWAYS ADDS SOME GRATED PARMESAN CHEESE FOR THAT EXTRA LITTLE ZING!
OH, MAN! LOOKS LIKE THEY'RE FIXING TO COOK HOMER!
QUICK! NO ONE IS WATCHING! LET'S ESCAPE.
WOO-HOO!!!
I HAVE A PLAN TO GET SPRINGFIELD OUT OF THIS MESS.
I'M ALL EARS!
CUT THE CORN.
IT WAS JUST A LITTLE WORD PLAY.
NO! THAT'S MY IDEA: CUT THE CORN! IT'S THE CORN THAT HAS TURNED ALL THE KIDS INTO ZOMBIES. WE'LL GET GROUNDSKEEPER WILLIE TO CUT IT DOWN AND THAT WILL BREAK THE SPELL!

GROUNDSKEEPER WILLIE! WE'VE GOT TO SAVE THE CHILDREN!
ETHAN ALL AND HIS EVIL CORN HAS THEM ALL HYPNOTIZED!
OCH! DEVIL CORN, IS IT? I THOUGHT THE WEE LADS AND LASSIES WERE ACTING A BIT TETCHED IN THE HEAD.
IT'S LIKE THEIR BRAINS HAVE BEEN WASHED OR DRY CLEANED OR SOME-THING! WE'VE GOT TO DESTROY THE CORNFIELDS!
SAY NO MORE! JUST LEAVE THINGS TO ME TRUSTY TRACTOR AND ME LADY LOVE, SUPER LEADED ETHYL!
GASOLINE
GOD BLESS FOSSIL FUELS!
THAT'S IS SO NOT THE MORAL OF THIS STORY, BART.
♪ MOWING DOWN THE CORN. MOWING DOWN THE CORN. WE WILL COME REJOICING MOWING DOWN THE CORN. ♪

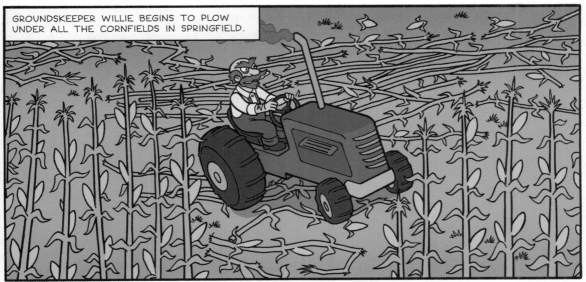

GROUNDSKEEPER WILLIE BEGINS TO PLOW UNDER ALL THE CORNFIELDS IN SPRINGFIELD.

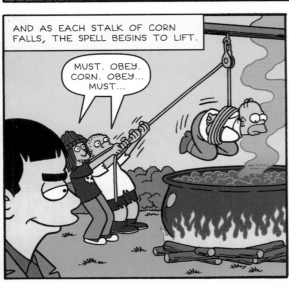

AND AS EACH STALK OF CORN FALLS, THE SPELL BEGINS TO LIFT.

MUST. OBEY. CORN. OBEY... MUST...

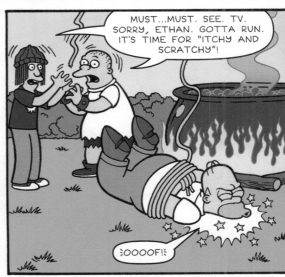

MUST...MUST. SEE. TV. SORRY, ETHAN. GOTTA RUN. IT'S TIME FOR "ITCHY AND SCRATCHY"!

≶OOOOF!≶

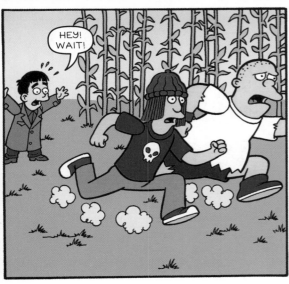

HEY! WAIT!

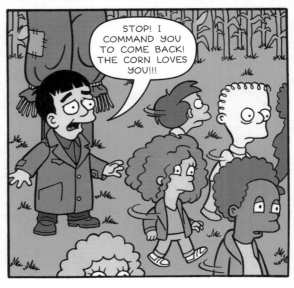

STOP! I COMMAND YOU TO COME BACK! THE CORN LOVES YOU!!!

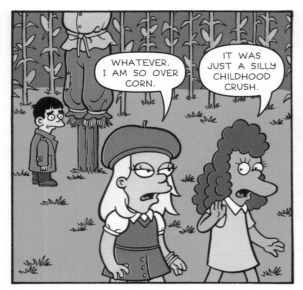

WHATEVER. I AM SO OVER CORN.

IT WAS JUST A SILLY CHILDHOOD CRUSH.

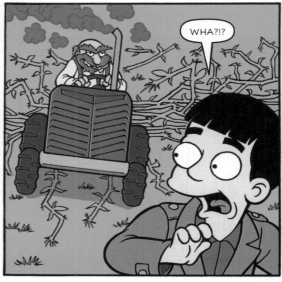

WHA?!?

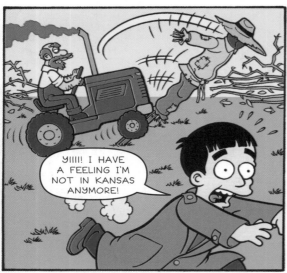

YIIII! I HAVE A FEELING I'M NOT IN KANSAS ANYMORE!

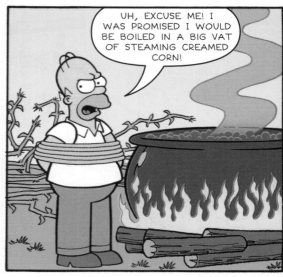

UH, EXCUSE ME! I WAS PROMISED I WOULD BE BOILED IN A BIG VAT OF STEAMING CREAMED CORN!

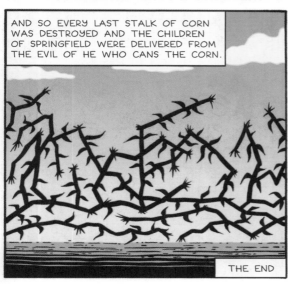

AND SO EVERY LAST STALK OF CORN WAS DESTROYED AND THE CHILDREN OF SPRINGFIELD WERE DELIVERED FROM THE EVIL OF HE WHO CANS THE CORN.

THE END

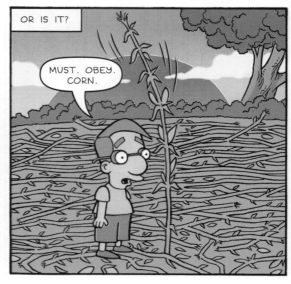

OR IS IT?

MUST. OBEY. CORN.

MAGGIE'S CRIB

by ARAGONÉS

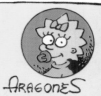

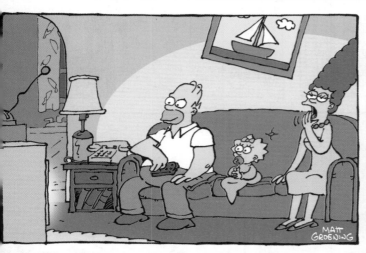

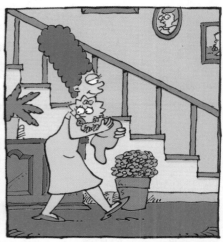

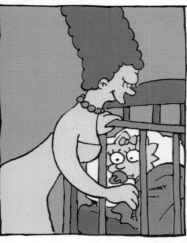

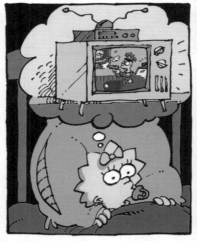

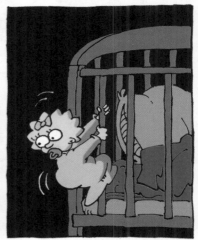

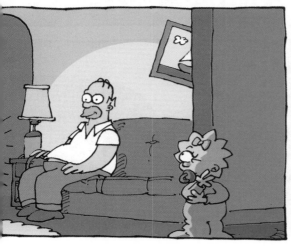

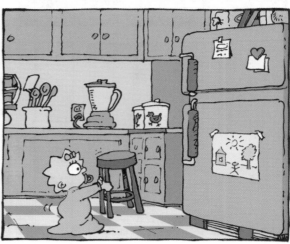

SERGIO ARAGONÉS
SCRIPT & ART

JACOB GLASER
COLORS

BILL MORRISON
EDITOR

PSHTT
SLAM!
ARAGONÉS 09

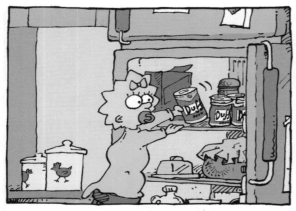

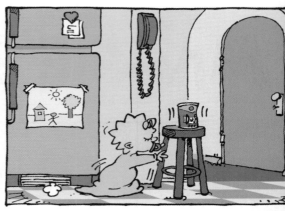

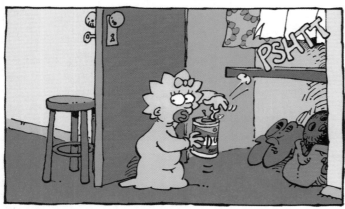

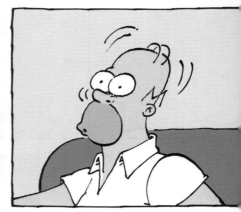

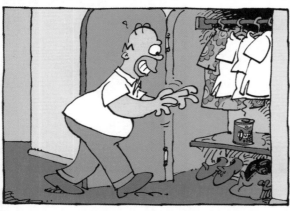

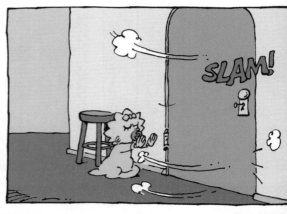

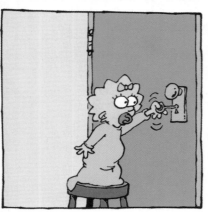

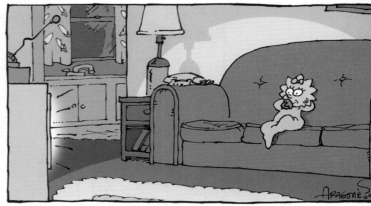

BART SIMPSON'S GUIDE TO

YOU CAN LEAD A BART TO SCHOOL, BUT YOU CAN'T MAKE ME LEARN!

THE LAST DAY OF SUMMER VACATION

MATT GROENING

REMEMBER, THERE'S ONLY ONE LAST DAY OF SUMMER VACATION, AND YOU DON'T WANT TO WASTE IT. SLEEP AS LATE AS POSSIBLE.

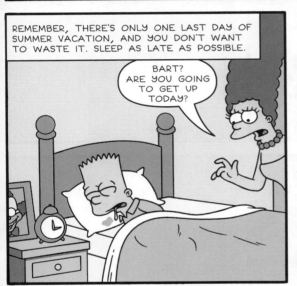

BART? ARE YOU GOING TO GET UP TODAY?

MAKE SURE YOU WEAR YOUR OLDEST AND MOST COMFORTABLE CLOTHES. AND THE STINKIER, THE BETTER.

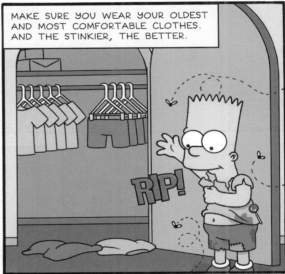

RIP!

EAT A BOX OF COOKIES FOR LUNCH.

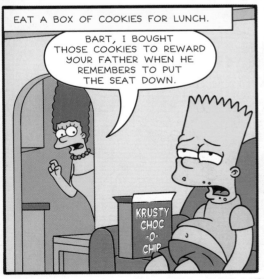

BART, I BOUGHT THOSE COOKIES TO REWARD YOUR FATHER WHEN HE REMEMBERS TO PUT THE SEAT DOWN.

KRUSTY CHOC -O- CHIP

GET ALL THE IMPORTANT SCHOOL SUPPLIES READY FOR THE NEW YEAR.

WHAT HAPPENED TO MY EGGS? HOMER MUST'VE BEEN IN A MOOD FOR OMELET-PALOOZA THIS MORNING.

SKINNER KRABAPPEL MOE FLANDERS MOLEMAN

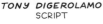
TONY DIGEROLAMO
SCRIPT

JOEY NILGES
PENCILS

MIKE ROTE
INKS

ROBERT STANLEY
COLORS

KAREN BATES
LETTERS

BILL MORRISON
EDITOR

FILL YOUR BRAIN WITH AS MUCH COMIC BOOK TRIVIA AS POSSIBLE, LEAVING NO ROOM FOR SCHOOL LEARNIN'.

PLAY VIDEO GAMES UNTIL MAXIMUM EYE STRAIN IS ACHIEVED.

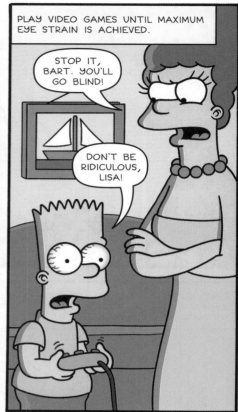

STOP IT, BART. YOU'LL GO BLIND!

DON'T BE RIDICULOUS, LISA!

IT'S A BRAND NEW YEAR, SO BE SURE TO TEST YOUR NEW MATERIAL.

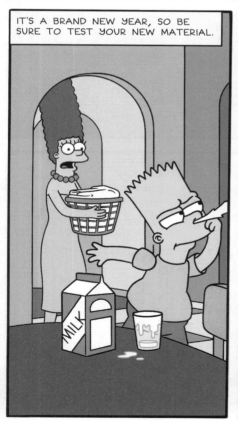

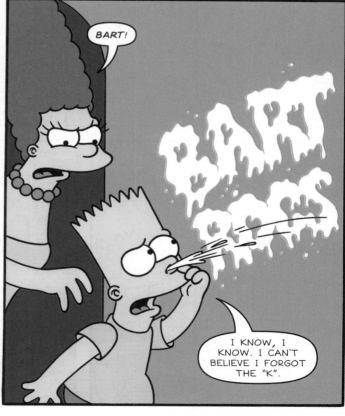

BART!

I KNOW, I KNOW. I CAN'T BELIEVE I FORGOT THE "K".

GIVE YOUR DOG ONE LAST REALLY GOOD WORKOUT.
CRASH!
BOOM!
BANG!
HRMMM... **OUTSIDE,** YOU TWO!
HRMMM... GET **IN HERE,** YOU TWO!
BANG!
CRASH!
BOOM!
GO HAMPER SURFING ONE LAST TIME.
CRASH!
MY **HAMPER!**

GET RID OF THOSE BOTHERSOME TAN LINES.
MOM, CAN YOU GET MY BACK?
OH, LORD. PUT SOME CLOTHES ON!
MAN, I WISH *EVERY* DAY WAS THE LAST DAY OF SUMMER VACATION.
WELL, IT *ISN'T*! STARTING TOMORROW, I'VE GOT FIVE STRAIGHT DAYS UNTIL SATURDAY TO RELAX.
HEY, THAT'S RIGHT! I HAVEN'T DONE ANYTHING TODAY THAT I CAN'T DO ON THE *WEEKEND*!
THANKS, MOM!
SCRUB
SCRUB
BUZZ
BUZZ
SIGH
THE END

12 ANGRY KIDS
NOOOO!
MATT GROENING
WHAT'S WRONG, SEYMOUR?
SOMEONE PICKED THE LOCK TO MY OFFICE DOOR AND STOLE MY COLLECTION OF WAR MEDALS!
NELSON MUNTZ!
HUH?
GIVE ME BACK MY WAR MEDALS!
WHAT?
DON'T PLAY DUMB. I KNOW YOU TOOK THEM.

JAMES W. BATES SCRIPT — *MIKE KAZALEH* PENCILS — *PHYLLIS NOVIN* INKS — *ART VILLANUEVA* COLORS — *KAREN BATES* LETTERS — *BILL MORRISON* EDITOR

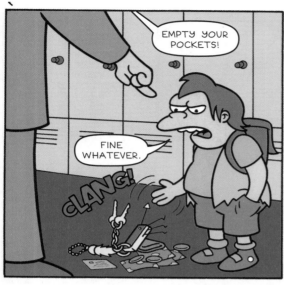

EMPTY YOUR POCKETS!

FINE WHATEVER.

CLANG!

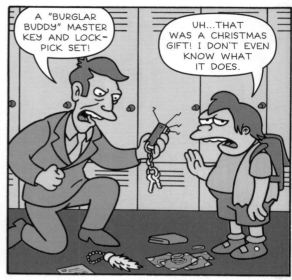

A "BURGLAR BUDDY" MASTER KEY AND LOCK-PICK SET!

UH...THAT WAS A CHRISTMAS GIFT! I DON'T EVEN KNOW WHAT IT DOES.

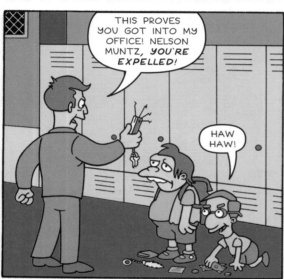

THIS PROVES YOU GOT INTO MY OFFICE! NELSON MUNTZ, *YOU'RE EXPELLED!*

HAW HAW!

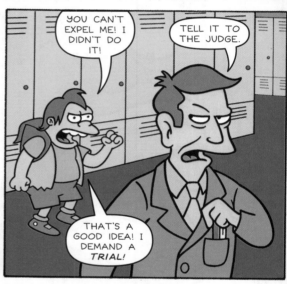

YOU CAN'T EXPEL ME! I DIDN'T DO IT!

TELL IT TO THE JUDGE.

THAT'S A GOOD IDEA! I DEMAND A *TRIAL!*

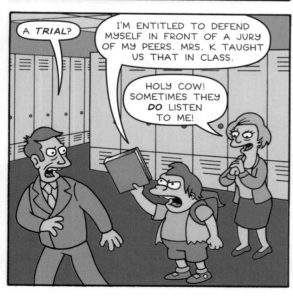

A *TRIAL?*

I'M ENTITLED TO DEFEND MYSELF IN FRONT OF A JURY OF MY PEERS. MRS. K TAUGHT US THAT IN CLASS.

HOLY COW! SOMETIMES THEY *DO* LISTEN TO ME!

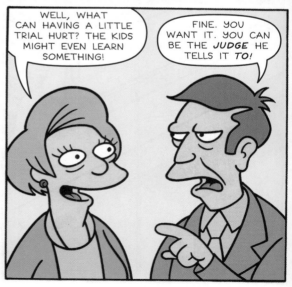

WELL, WHAT CAN HAVING A LITTLE TRIAL HURT? THE KIDS MIGHT EVEN LEARN SOMETHING!

FINE. YOU WANT IT. YOU CAN BE THE *JUDGE* HE TELLS IT *TO!*

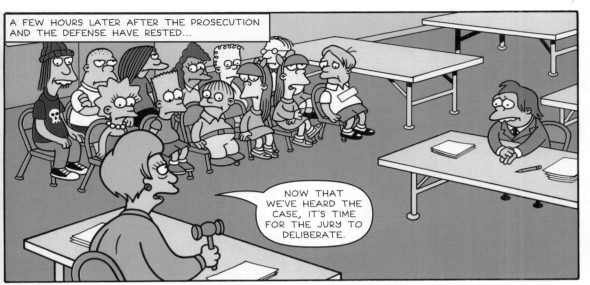

A FEW HOURS LATER AFTER THE PROSECUTION AND THE DEFENSE HAVE RESTED...

NOW THAT WE'VE HEARD THE CASE, IT'S TIME FOR THE JURY TO DELIBERATE.

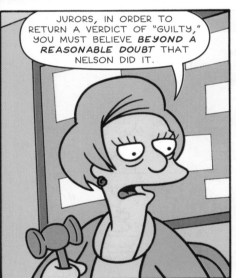

JURORS, IN ORDER TO RETURN A VERDICT OF "GUILTY," YOU MUST BELIEVE *BEYOND A REASONABLE DOUBT* THAT NELSON DID IT.

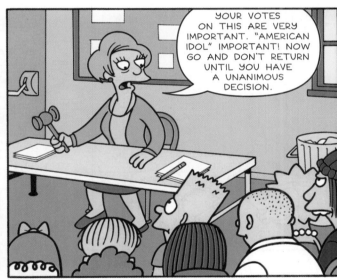

YOUR VOTES ON THIS ARE VERY IMPORTANT. "AMERICAN IDOL" IMPORTANT! NOW GO AND DON'T RETURN UNTIL YOU HAVE A UNANIMOUS DECISION.

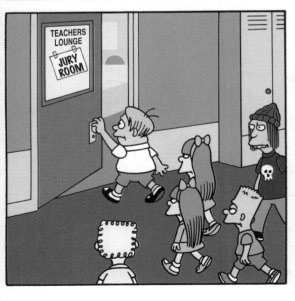

TEACHERS LOUNGE

JURY ROOM

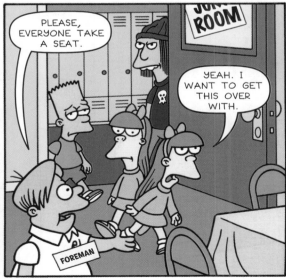

JURY ROOM

PLEASE, EVERYONE TAKE A SEAT.

YEAH. I WANT TO GET THIS OVER WITH.

FOREMAN

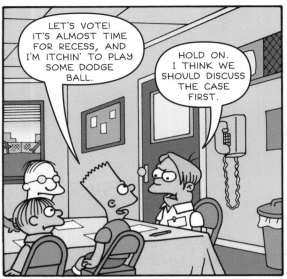

LET'S VOTE! IT'S ALMOST TIME FOR RECESS, AND I'M ITCHIN' TO PLAY SOME DODGE BALL.

HOLD ON. I THINK WE SHOULD DISCUSS THE CASE FIRST.

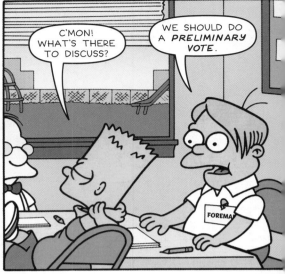

C'MON! WHAT'S THERE TO DISCUSS?

WE SHOULD DO A *PRELIMINARY VOTE*.

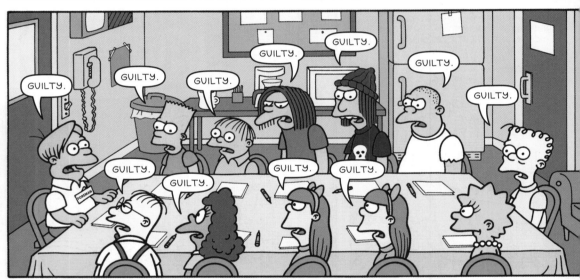

GUILTY.

GUILTY.

GUILTY.

GUILTY.

GUILTY.

GUILTY.

GUILTY.

GUILTY.

GUILTY.

GUILTY.

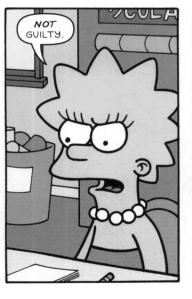

NOT GUILTY.

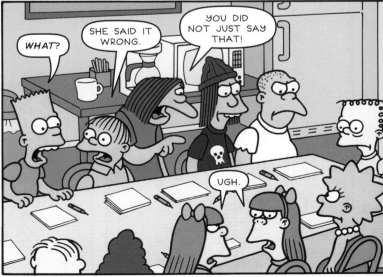

WHAT?

SHE SAID IT WRONG.

YOU DID NOT JUST SAY THAT!

UGH.

62

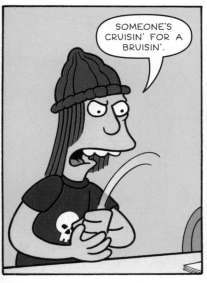

SOMEONE'S CRUISIN' FOR A BRUISIN'.

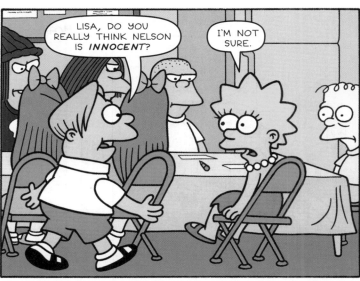

LISA, DO YOU REALLY THINK NELSON IS *INNOCENT*?

I'M NOT SURE.

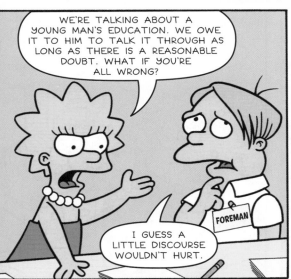

WE'RE TALKING ABOUT A YOUNG MAN'S EDUCATION. WE OWE IT TO HIM TO TALK IT THROUGH AS LONG AS THERE IS A REASONABLE DOUBT. WHAT IF YOU'RE ALL WRONG?

I GUESS A LITTLE DISCOURSE WOULDN'T HURT.

FOREMAN

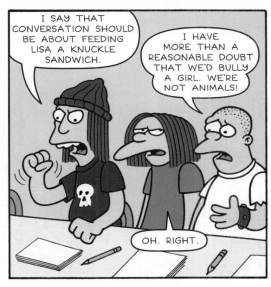

I SAY THAT CONVERSATION SHOULD BE ABOUT FEEDING LISA A KNUCKLE SANDWICH.

I HAVE MORE THAN A REASONABLE DOUBT THAT WE'D BULLY A GIRL. WE'RE NOT ANIMALS!

OH. RIGHT.

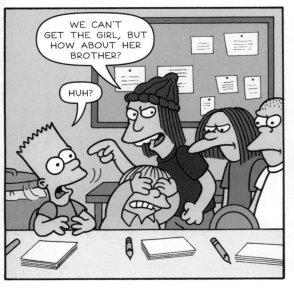

WE CAN'T GET THE GIRL, BUT HOW ABOUT HER BROTHER?

HUH?

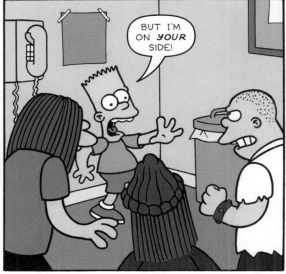

BUT I'M ON *YOUR* SIDE!

WHAT DO YOU SAY, LISA?
I SAY THE CASE AGAINST NELSON ISN'T STRONG ENOUGH TO PROVE HE'S GUILTY BEYOND A REASONABLE DOUBT!
OUCH!
WE GAVE HIM A TRIAL.
A FAIR TRIAL.
ARE WE GIVING HIM A FAIR TRIAL?
IS IT FAIR THAT NONE OF YOU ARE TAKING THIS SERIOUSLY?
HEY! GIVE BACK WIGGLE PUPPY!
RALPH, WHY DO YOU THINK NELSON IS GUILTY?
BECAUSE EVERYONE ELSE DOES.
WENDELL?
I DON'T KNOW. I JUST DO.
NELSON HAS PILFERED MILK MONEY FROM MANY OF US OVER THE YEARS.
FOREMAN

NELSON'S A BAD EGG. TRUST US. ***WE*** COME FROM THE SAME CARTON.
C'MON, JUST VOTE "GUILTY."
NO...NOT UNTIL SOMEONE CONVINCES ME.
HAVE IT YOUR WAY.
BART, WE'RE GONNA INTRODUCE YOUR HEAD TO MR. TOILET.
IT'S SWIRLY TIME!
LISA!
THE ONLY EVIDENCE IS THE LOCK-PICK SET.
ONLY EVIDENCE? THAT'S PRETTY CONVINCING.
IS IT?
FLUSH!
DOES ANYONE ***HERE*** HAVE A "BURGLAR BUDDY" ***OR*** A COPY OF THE SCHOOL'S MASTER KEY?
'FESS UP!
HERE.
I THOUGHT ***EVERYONE*** HAD ONE OF THESE.
OCCUPATIONAL NECESSITY.
I KEEP AN EXTRA ONE IN MY LOCKER.
DADDY MADE ME A MASTER KEY. I GET TRAPPED SOMETIMES.
FOREMAN
A JUNIOR CAMPER SHOULD ALWAYS "BE PREPARED!"

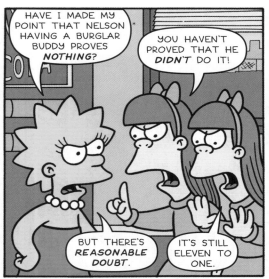

HAVE I MADE MY POINT THAT NELSON HAVING A BURGLAR BUDDY PROVES *NOTHING*?

YOU HAVEN'T PROVED THAT HE *DIDN'T* DO IT!

BUT THERE'S *REASONABLE DOUBT*.

IT'S STILL ELEVEN TO ONE.

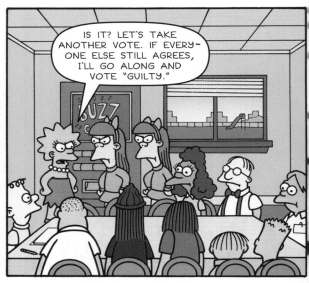

IS IT? LET'S TAKE ANOTHER VOTE. IF EVERY- ONE ELSE STILL AGREES, I'LL GO ALONG AND VOTE "GUILTY."

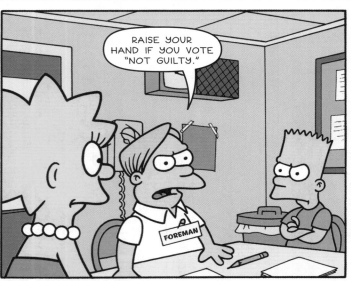

RAISE YOUR HAND IF YOU VOTE "NOT GUILTY."

FOREMAN

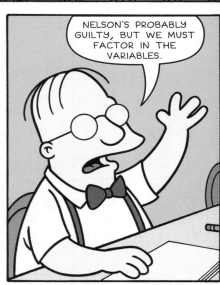

NELSON'S PROBABLY GUILTY, BUT WE MUST FACTOR IN THE VARIABLES.

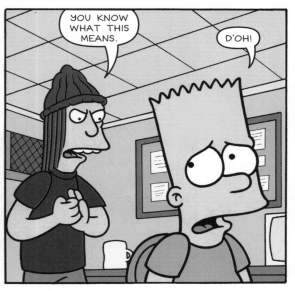

YOU KNOW WHAT THIS MEANS.

D'OH!

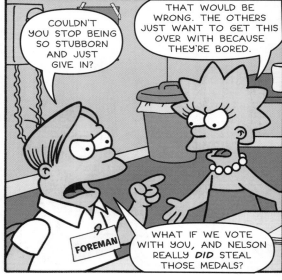

COULDN'T YOU STOP BEING SO STUBBORN AND JUST GIVE IN?

THAT WOULD BE WRONG. THE OTHERS JUST WANT TO GET THIS OVER WITH BECAUSE THEY'RE BORED.

FOREMAN

WHAT IF WE VOTE WITH YOU, AND NELSON REALLY *DID* STEAL THOSE MEDALS?

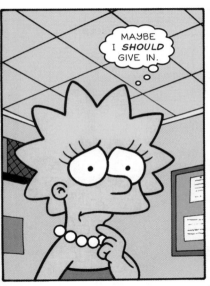

MAYBE I *SHOULD* GIVE IN.

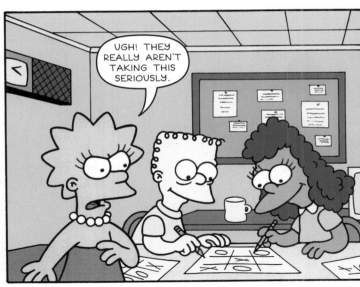

UGH! THEY REALLY AREN'T TAKING THIS SERIOUSLY.

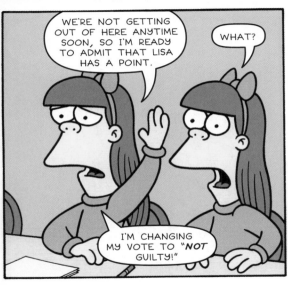

WE'RE NOT GETTING OUT OF HERE ANYTIME SOON, SO I'M READY TO ADMIT THAT LISA HAS A POINT.

WHAT?

I'M CHANGING MY VOTE TO "*NOT* GUILTY!"

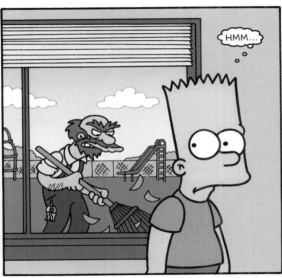

HMM...

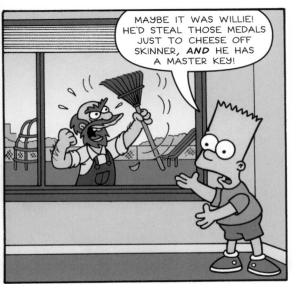

MAYBE IT WAS WILLIE! HE'D STEAL THOSE MEDALS JUST TO CHEESE OFF SKINNER, *AND* HE HAS A MASTER KEY!

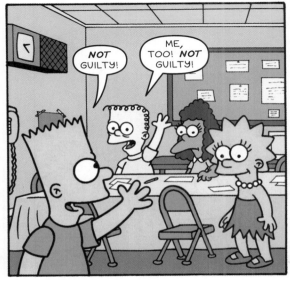

NOT GUILTY!

ME, TOO! *NOT* GUILTY!

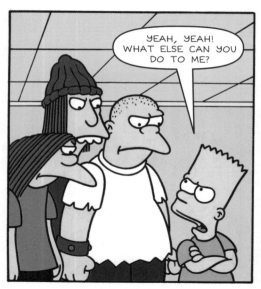

YEAH, YEAH! WHAT ELSE CAN YOU DO TO ME?

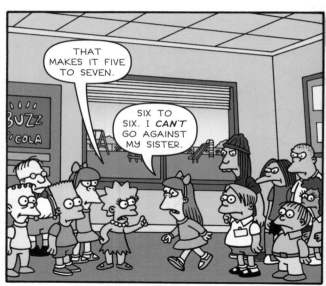

THAT MAKES IT FIVE TO SEVEN.

SIX TO SIX. I *CAN'T* GO AGAINST MY SISTER.

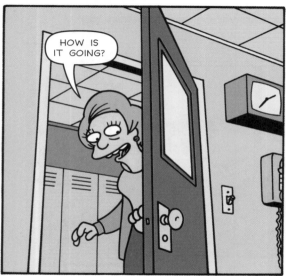

HOW IS IT GOING?

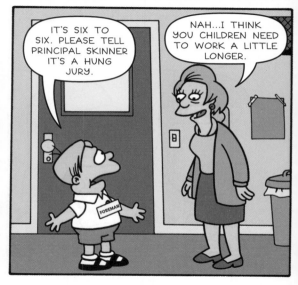

IT'S SIX TO SIX. PLEASE TELL PRINCIPAL SKINNER IT'S A HUNG JURY.

NAH...I THINK YOU CHILDREN NEED TO WORK A LITTLE LONGER.

FOREMAN

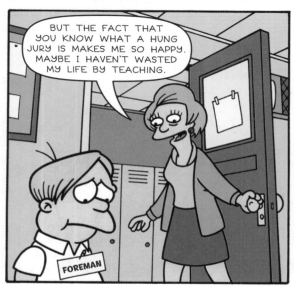

BUT THE FACT THAT YOU KNOW WHAT A HUNG JURY IS MAKES ME SO HAPPY. MAYBE I HAVEN'T WASTED MY LIFE BY TEACHING.

FOREMAN

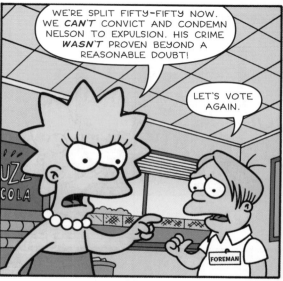

WE'RE SPLIT FIFTY-FIFTY NOW. WE *CAN'T* CONVICT AND CONDEMN NELSON TO EXPULSION. HIS CRIME *WASN'T* PROVEN BEYOND A REASONABLE DOUBT!

LET'S VOTE AGAIN.

FOREMAN

RAISE YOUR HAND IF YOU VOTE "NOT GUILTY."
FOREMAN
WAIT!
YOU THREE KNOW BETTER THAN ANYBODY HOW UNFAIR IT IS WHEN PEOPLE AUTO-MATICALLY ASSUME YOU'RE GUILTY.
YEAH, BUT I ALWAYS AM GUILTY.
I GET BLAMED FOR STUFF I DIDN'T DO ALL THE TIME. I'LL CHANGE MY VOTE.
ME, TOO. NOT GUILTY.
TRAITORS!
IT'S ELEVEN TO ONE. WHAT DO YOU SAY?
BUZZ

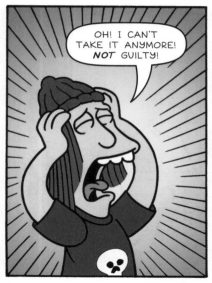

OH! I CAN'T TAKE IT ANYMORE! *NOT* GUILTY!

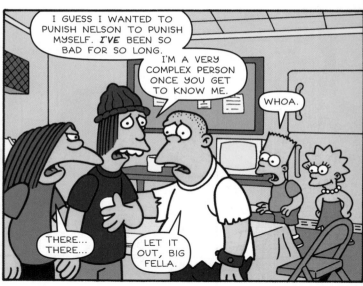

I GUESS I WANTED TO PUNISH NELSON TO PUNISH MYSELF. *I'VE* BEEN SO BAD FOR SO LONG.

I'M A VERY COMPLEX PERSON ONCE YOU GET TO KNOW ME.

WHOA.

THERE... THERE...

LET IT OUT, BIG FELLA.

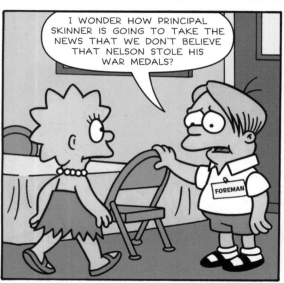

I WONDER HOW PRINCIPAL SKINNER IS GOING TO TAKE THE NEWS THAT WE DON'T BELIEVE THAT NELSON STOLE HIS WAR MEDALS?

FOREMAN

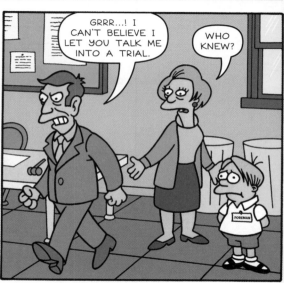

GRRR...! I CAN'T BELIEVE I LET YOU TALK ME INTO A TRIAL.

WHO KNEW?

FOREMAN

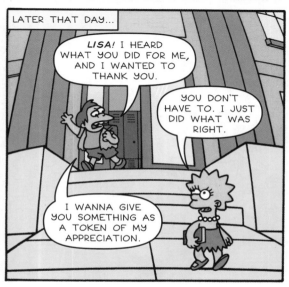

LATER THAT DAY...

LISA! I HEARD WHAT YOU DID FOR ME, AND I WANTED TO THANK YOU.

YOU DON'T HAVE TO. I JUST DID WHAT WAS RIGHT.

I WANNA GIVE YOU SOMETHING AS A TOKEN OF MY APPRECIATION.

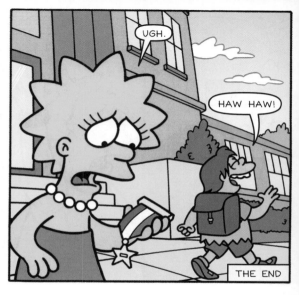

UGH.

HAW HAW!

THE END

MAGGIE'S CRIB

by ARAGONÉS

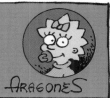

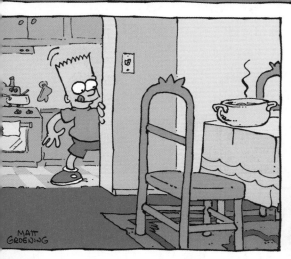

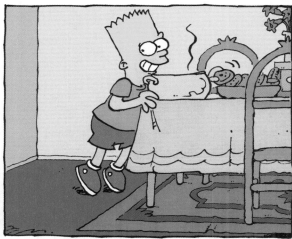

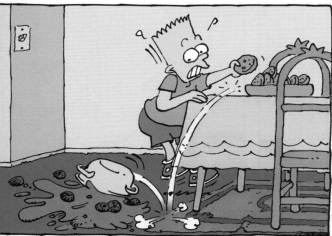

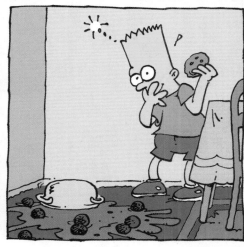

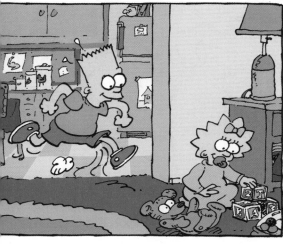

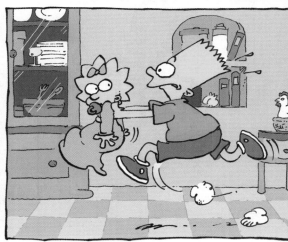

SERGIO ARAGONÉS
STORY & ART

ART VILLANUEVA
COLORS

BILL MORRISON
EDITOR

Li'L KRUSTY

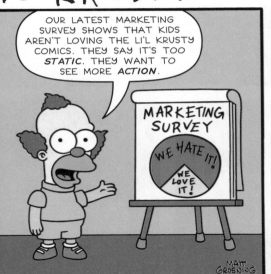

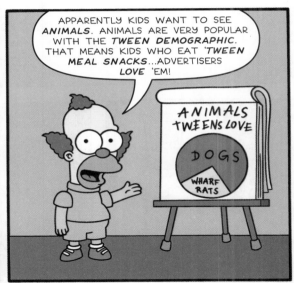

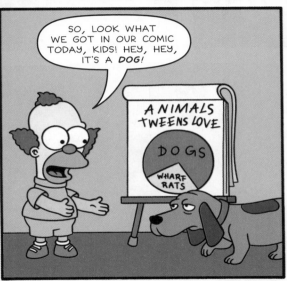

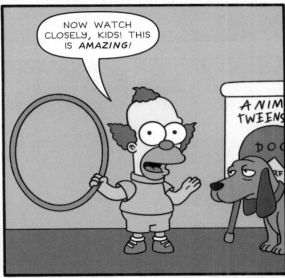

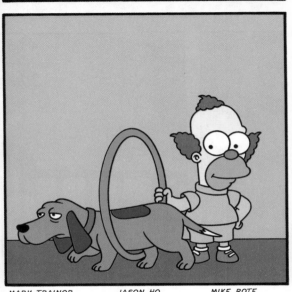

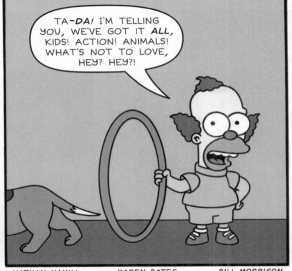

MARY TRAINOR
SCRIPT

JASON HO
PENCILS

MIKE ROTE
INKS

NATHAN HAMILL
COLORS

KAREN BATES
LETTERS

BILL MORRISON
EDITOR

MAGGIE'S CRIB

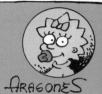

by ARAGONÉS

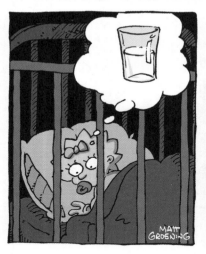

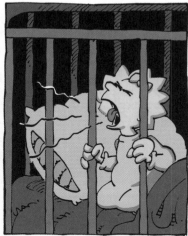

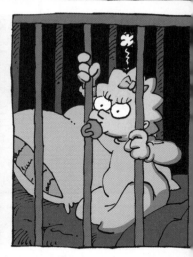

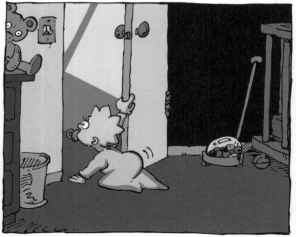

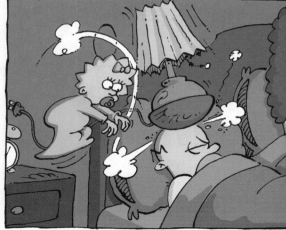

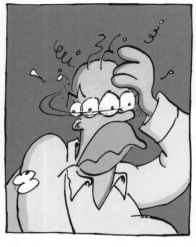

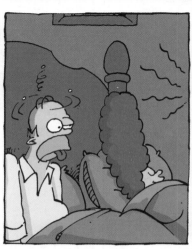

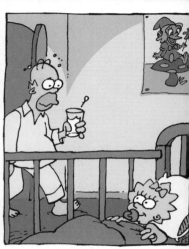

SERGIO ARAGONÉS
SCRIPT & ART

JACOB GLASER
COLORS

BILL MORRISON
EDITOR

HOMER SIMPSON: CHICK MAGNET

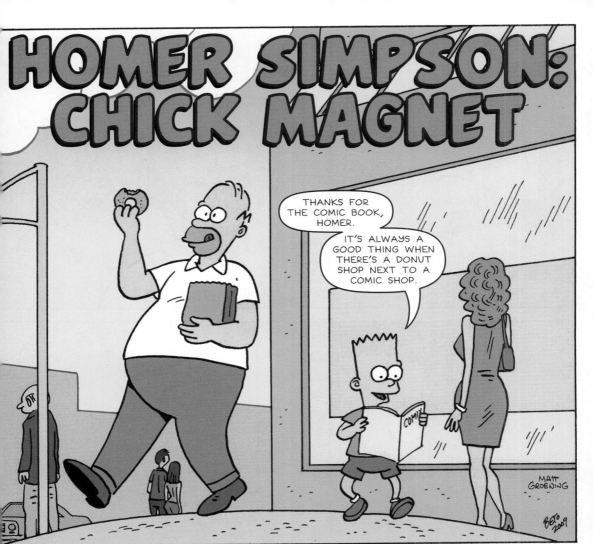

THANKS FOR THE COMIC BOOK, HOMER.

IT'S ALWAYS A GOOD THING WHEN THERE'S A DONUT SHOP NEXT TO A COMIC SHOP.

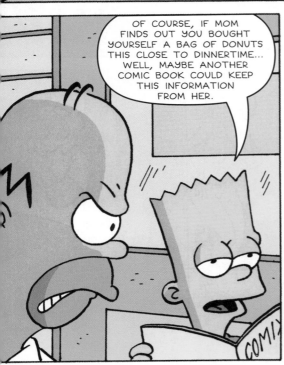

OF COURSE, IF MOM FINDS OUT YOU BOUGHT YOURSELF A BAG OF DONUTS THIS CLOSE TO DINNERTIME... WELL, MAYBE ANOTHER COMIC BOOK COULD KEEP THIS INFORMATION FROM HER.

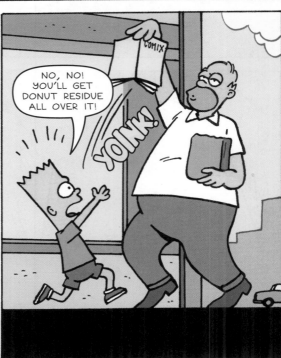

NO, NO! YOU'LL GET DONUT RESIDUE ALL OVER IT!

YOINK!

GILBERT HERNANDEZ
STORY & ART

ALAN HELLARD
COLORS

KAREN BATES
LETTERS

BILL MORRISON
EDITOR

TWO POINTS!
SACRILEGE!
YOU WATCH MY BACK, I WATCH YOURS.
SEE? NO COMIC!
YEAH, IT'S A RUINED COMIC BOOK NOW, BUT WE HAVE TO MAKE THESE SACRIFICES SOMETIMES.

EXCUSE ME SIR, BUT I--
I'M INNOCENT!
I COULDN'T HELP NOTICING...
THAT WHEN THE LIGHT HITS YOU A CERTAIN WAY...
YOU'RE...
...HANDSOME.
OH, THAT!
BART.
WELL, YOU'RE A FEW YEARS TOO LATE, LADY.
DAD'S A HAPPILY MARRIED MAN...HUH, HOMER?
BART.
BUT YOU DON'T UNDERSTAND...I'M A VERY INFLUENTIAL FILM PRODUCER.
BARRRT!
YEAH, AND HOMER AND I ARE FAMOUS TV STARS.
SO WHAT IF SHE WAS ONLY GIVING US A LINE...?!
REMEMBER, HOMER, I DON'T HAVE A COMIC BOOK, AND YOU'VE GOT DONUTS.

I GUESS SHE ***WAS*** KINDA PRETTY.
NOT LIKE YOUR MOTHER, PAL.
EWW, NORMALLY THAT CUTESY CUTE STUFF MAKES ME WANT TO HURL, BUT IN THIS CASE...
SIR!
OH, SIR!
OH YES, OF COURSE, YOU MUST BE A TV STAR!
GULP.
MERCHANDISING AND EVERYTHING, LADY!
MY CHILD IS AN ASPIRING TV STAR AS WELL!
SHOW THEM, AMOUR!
♪ JEEPERS ♫ CREEPERS, WHERE'D YOU GET THOSE ♫ PEEPERS? ♪

♪ JEEPERS ♫ CREEPERS, WHERE'D YOU GET THOSE ♫ EYES? ♪
WELL, IF MY NAME ISN'T HOMER SIMPSON.
UH, HOMER, YOU MIGHT NOT WANT TO MENTION THAT IN FRONT OF THEM.
HOMER... SIMP--
ZOOM!
BOY, SHE WAS OUT OF HERE LIKE A LOCUST!
WHAT A DAY.
BUMP!
NO, WAIT.
DON'T TELL ME.
OK, IF YOU INSIST.

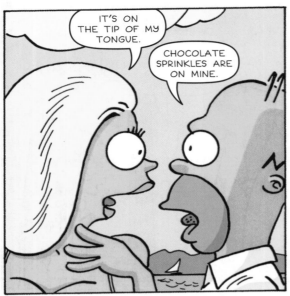

IT'S ON THE TIP OF MY TONGUE.

CHOCOLATE SPRINKLES ARE ON MINE.

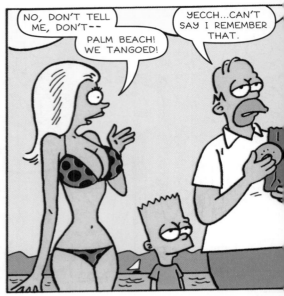

NO, DON'T TELL ME, DON'T-- PALM BEACH! WE TANGOED!

YECCH...CAN'T SAY I REMEMBER THAT.

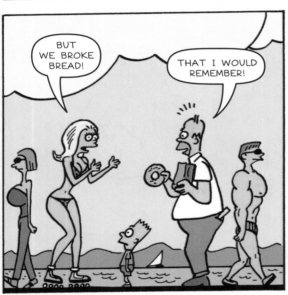

BUT WE BROKE BREAD!

THAT I WOULD REMEMBER!

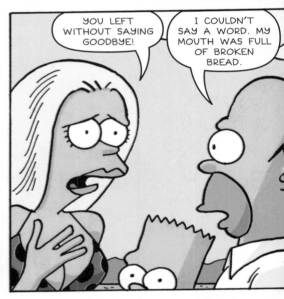

YOU LEFT WITHOUT SAYING GOODBYE!

I COULDN'T SAY A WORD. MY MOUTH WAS FULL OF BROKEN BREAD.

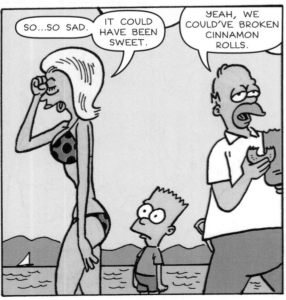

SO...SO SAD.

IT COULD HAVE BEEN SWEET.

YEAH, WE COULD'VE BROKEN CINNAMON ROLLS.

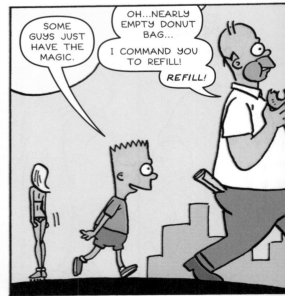

SOME GUYS JUST HAVE THE MAGIC.

OH...NEARLY EMPTY DONUT BAG...

I COMMAND YOU TO REFILL!

REFILL!

NOW I'M INTRIGUED WITH ALL THESE WOMEN.
HOW ABOUT A TEST?
BRING 'ER ON!
HI!
MEET MY DAD!
WHY?
WELL HOMER, YOU CAN'T WIN 'EM ALL!
WAIT!
I DIDN'T KNOW!
YOU'RE NOT LIKE THE REST, ARE YA?
THUMP!
UH...NICE MEETING YOU.
WAIT, YOU MIGHT HAVE WHAT IT TAKES!
SLUG!

NEVER MET A MAN THAT COULD HANDLE ONE OF THESE!
OR A GOOD DOSE OF THIS!
HANG IN THERE, HOMER!
YOU'RE WEARING HER OUT!
UH-OH... NOT FOR PRYING EYES!
COMIX
OH WELL, YOU TURNED OUT JUST LIKE THE REST.
MY DONUTS...
WHERE--
AFTER THAT, YOU DESERVE 'EM!

I'M TEMPTED TO CONTINUE OUR EXPERIMENT IF YOU DON'T MIND, HOMER.
WERE WE EXPERIMENTING?
HI.
EXPERIMENT OVER!
I'M SURE IT'S ALL A COINCIDENCE AND WOMEN AREN'T BEING LURED BY A COMIC BOOK.
SHOVE!
HUH?
OH MY LORD, GIRLS...
LOOK!
OKAY, MAYBE IT'S AN EXTREMELY RARE EDITION.
?

THEN IT'S THE DONUTS. IT'S GOTTA BE THE--
UH, HOMER...

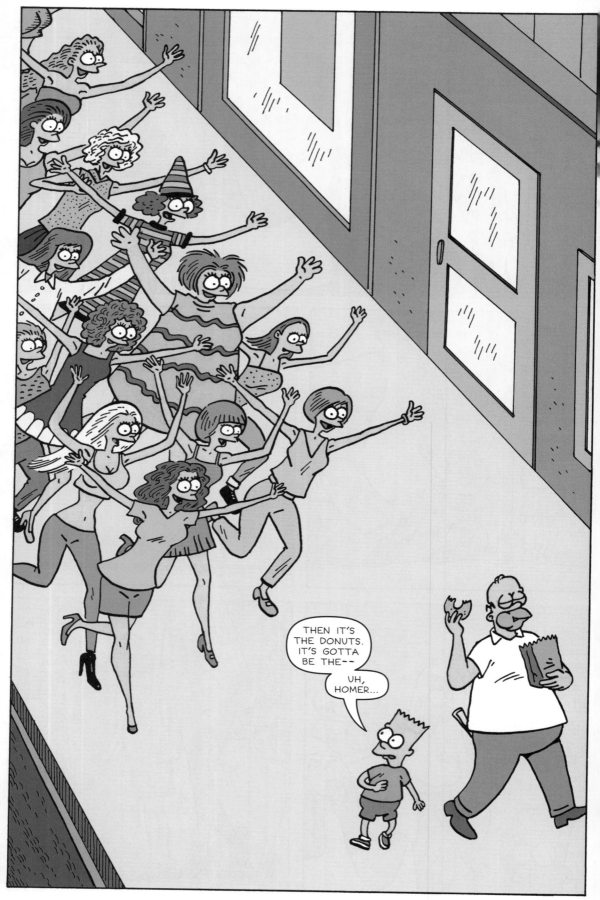

D'OH!
I ADMIT DEFEAT! THEY CAN HAVE IT!
COMIX
HERE, AND I HOPE YOU GET A LOUSY DEAL ON EBUY!
LOOK. NO INTEREST.
IT CAN ONLY MEAN ONE THING, AND IT AIN'T DONUTS.

A MAN WITH A COMIC BOOK ATTRACTS A WOMAN LIKE NOTHING ELSE, SO I MUST WARN ALL MEN OF THIS DANGEROUS REVELATION!
WHAT'S NEXT? THE THREE STOOGES?
CAN ANYONE TELL ME WHAT BART IS TALKING ABOUT?
WELL, AFTER YOU TWO BEING OUT ALL DAY, MAYBE YOU COULD USE A SNACK.
SURE, HOMER. YOU MUST BE FAMISHED!
I MUST'VE READ THE RECIPE WRONG, SO THERE'S A LITTLE EXTRA.
THIS'LL GO IN THE HISTORY BOOKS AS THE DAY HOMER REFUSED DONUTS.
ARE YOU SURE?
D'OH NUTS!
FILL IN THE BLANK!
The End

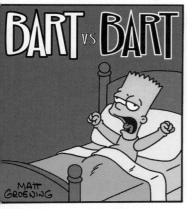 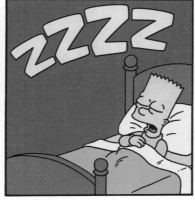 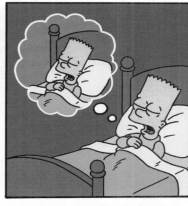

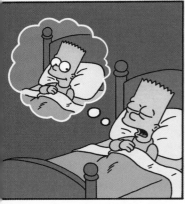 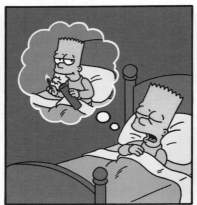 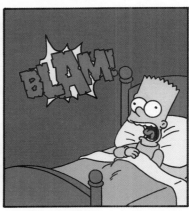

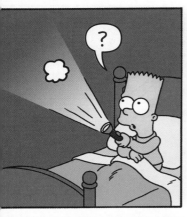 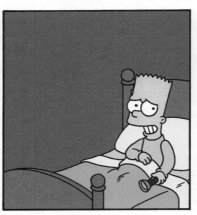 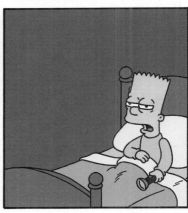

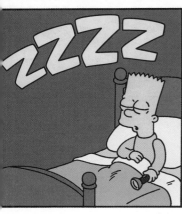 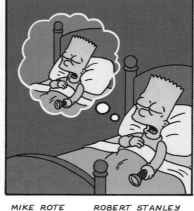 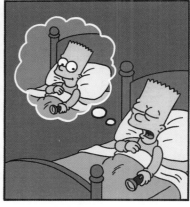

MARY TRAINOR
SCRIPT & LAYOUTS

JASON HO
PENCILS

MIKE ROTE
INKS

ROBERT STANLEY
COLORS

KAREN BATES
LETTERS

BILL MORRISON
EDITOR

WHA?
POP!
ZZZZ

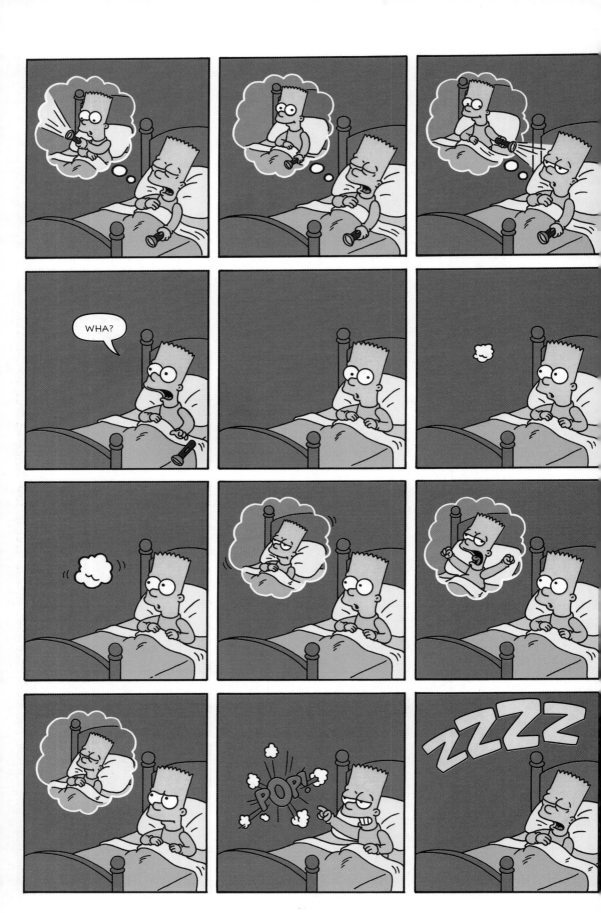

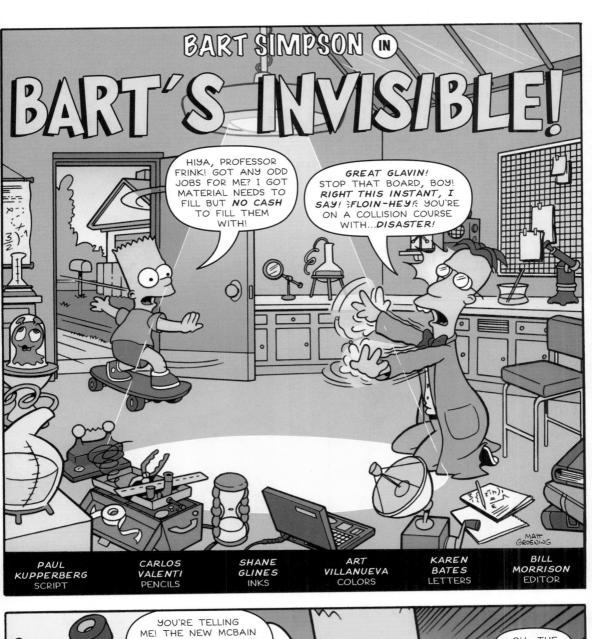

BART SIMPSON IN
BART'S INVISIBLE!

PAUL KUPPERBERG
SCRIPT

CARLOS VALENTI
PENCILS

SHANE GLINES
INKS

ART VILLANUEVA
COLORS

KAREN BATES
LETTERS

BILL MORRISON
EDITOR

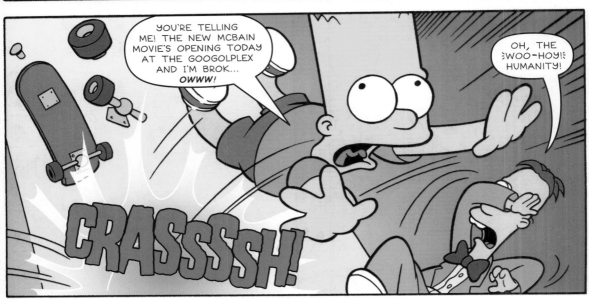

WHOA, DUDE! WH-WHAT HIT ME?
GREAT MARCONI, IT'S YOU WHO DID THE HITTING...WITH YOUR MULTI-WHEELED CONVEYANCE TRAVELING AT EXCESSIVE SPEED! GA-HEY!
HUH? WHAT'D I HIT?! THERE'S NOTHING HERE!
PRECISELY! AND NOW YOU HAVE BROKEN IT.
C'MON, PROFESSOR, IS THIS SOME KINDA JOKE OR...HUH?!
WELL, WHAT DO YOU KNOW? THERE IS SOME-THING HERE!
THAT'S WHAT I'VE BEEN SAYING. YOUR RECKLESSNESS HAS CAUSED GRIEVOUS DAMAGE TO MY INVISIBILITY MACHINE! ...OF COURSE, THUS FAR, IT HAS ONLY BEEN ABLE TO TURN ITSELF INVISIBLE... NILL-HEY
UH...IF IT'S INVISIBLE, HOW DO YOU KNOW I BUSTED IT?
OH. HEH-HEH.
CLATTER! CLATTER!

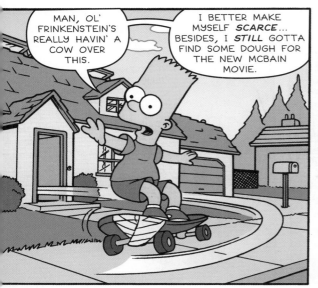

MAN, OL' FRINKENSTEIN'S REALLY HAVIN' A COW OVER THIS.

I BETTER MAKE MYSELF *SCARCE*... BESIDES, I *STILL* GOTTA FIND SOME DOUGH FOR THE NEW MCBAIN MOVIE.

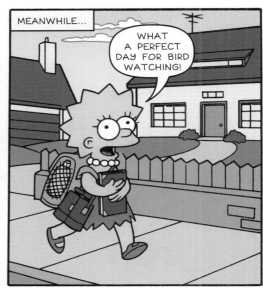

MEANWHILE...

WHAT A PERFECT DAY FOR BIRD WATCHING!

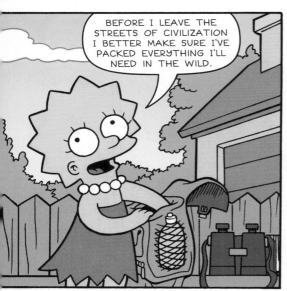

BEFORE I LEAVE THE STREETS OF CIVILIZATION I BETTER MAKE SURE I'VE PACKED EVERYTHING I'LL NEED IN THE WILD.

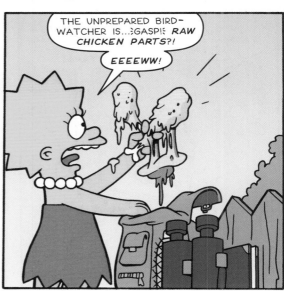

THE UNPREPARED BIRD-WATCHER IS...:GASP!: *RAW CHICKEN PARTS?!*

EEEEWW!

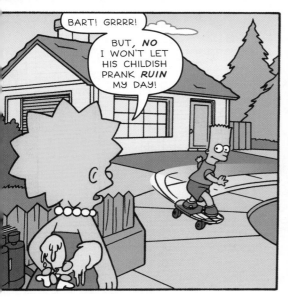

BART! GRRRR!

BUT, *NO* I WON'T LET HIS CHILDISH PRANK *RUIN* MY DAY!

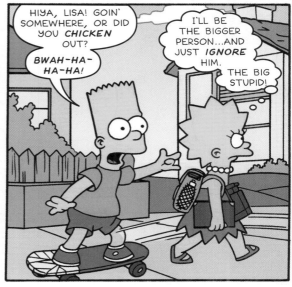

HIYA, LISA! GOIN' SOMEWHERE, OR DID YOU *CHICKEN* OUT?

BWAH-HA-HA-HA!

I'LL BE THE BIGGER PERSON...AND JUST *IGNORE* HIM.

THE BIG STUPID!

HEH! GUESS SHE FOUND MY LITTLE PRESENT...
...EITHER THAT, OR FRINKY'S MACHINE MADE ME INVISIBLE.
AS IF!
OH BOY! WE'VE SAVED OUR ALLOWANCE ALL MONTH FOR THIS!
THANK OUR HEAVENLY FATHER FOR DELICIOUS KRUSTY CHEW CANDY BARS!
AMEN!
OH NO! IT'S THE BLESSING-CHALLENGED BART SIMPSON!
HE'LL TRY TO TAKE OUR CANDY! WHAT SHOULD WE DO?!
HAR! NERDS AT TWELVE O'CLOCK LOCKING ON TARGET...!
THE GOOD LORD SAYS WE'RE SUPPOSED TO SHARE.
HE ALSO SAYS WE SHOULD TURN OUR OTHER CHEEKS. LET'S PRETEND HE'S NOT THERE.
AMEN!
WHAT'S THE WORD, GUYS? HEY, GUYS! GUYS?
HEY, WHAT IS IT WITH EVERYBODY TODAY?! MAYBE THEY DIDN'T HEAR ME.
OH WELL. MIGHT AS WELL GO HOME AND SEE IF I CAN CON HOMER OR MOM OUT OF THE PRICE OF A TICKET.

BART AND LISA ARE OUT, MAGGIE'S NAPPING, HOMER'S PASSED OUT ON THE SOFA...
...THE PERFECT TIME TO GET IN SOME SERIOUS HOUSECLEANING!
ZZZZZZZ
AND NOTHING GOES BETTER WITH THAT THAN THE MUSIC OF OINGO BOINGO, AS PERFORMED BY THE MELLOW 1,001 STRING ORCHESTRA!
♫ LA LA LA LA... ♪ WALKIN' WITH A DEAD MAN OVER MY SHOULDER... TRA-LA-LA-LA-LA...LEAVE YOUR BODY AT THE ♪ DOOR... ♫
MOM! CAN I HAVE MONEY FOR THE MOVIES. PLEASE, PLEASE, PLEASE, PLEASE!
BUT...MOM NEVER IGNORES MY PITIFUL LITTLE BOY VOICE!
UNLESS... SHE DOESN'T KNOW I'M HERE BECAUSE...
♪ ...WALKING WITH ♫ A DEAD MAN...LA-LA-DE-DA-LA-LA..DEAD ♫ MAN...DEAD ♪ MAN...
...BECAUSE THE FRINKSTER'S MACHINE REALLY DID MAKE ME INVISIBLE!
HUH? DID YOU SAY SOMETHING, BART?

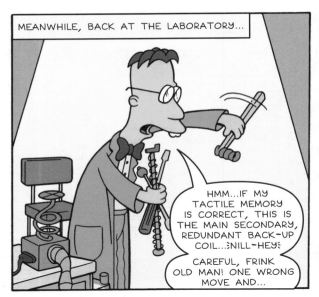

MEANWHILE, BACK AT THE LABORATORY...

HMM...IF MY TACTILE MEMORY IS CORRECT, THIS IS THE MAIN SECONDARY, REDUNDANT BACK-UP COIL...⁞NILL-HEY⁞

CAREFUL, FRINK OLD MAN! ONE WRONG MOVE AND...

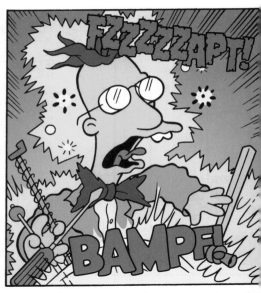

FZZZZZAPT!!

BAMPF!

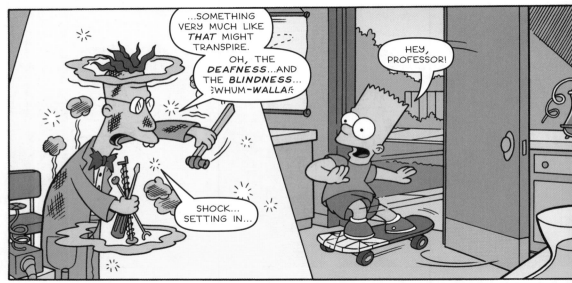

...SOMETHING VERY MUCH LIKE *THAT* MIGHT TRANSPIRE.

OH, THE *DEAFNESS*...AND THE *BLINDNESS*... ⁞WHUM-*WALLA*⁞

SHOCK... SETTING IN...

HEY, PROFESSOR!

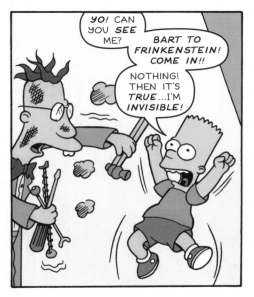

YO! CAN YOU *SEE* ME?

BART TO FRINKENSTEIN! COME IN!!

NOTHING! THEN IT'S *TRUE*...I'M *INVISIBLE!*

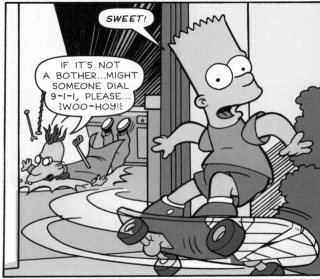

SWEET!

IF IT'S NOT A BOTHER...MIGHT SOMEONE DIAL 9-1-1, PLEASE... ⁞WOO-HOY⁞

SOON...
MAN, THIS IS BETTER THAN BEING GIVEN THE KEY TO THE CITY!
MY MCBAIN MOVIE MONEY PROBLEM IS SOLVED...
PANCAKE MIX
EGGS
MILK
...AND GRABBING SOME EATS TO ENJOY WITH THE FLICK IS NO PROBLEM-O EITHER!
EVERYBODY HANG IN THERE...I'VE SENT MY BEST MEN FOR MAPLE SYRUP!
ONE AT A TIME, GENTLEMEN, PLEASE! I AM NOT THE LORD SHIVA. I POSSESS BUT TWO ARMS!
AND WHAT IS YOUNG SIMPSON UP TO?
$3.98 + $3.98 + $1.99 + $2.49 + $0.98 + $4.49 + $2.25 + $1.49 = $21.65 + $1.30 SALES TAX = $22.95
CATCH YA LATER... SUCKER!
AH, SEEING I AM BUSY, HE HAS THOUGHTFULLY SHOWN ME HIS PURCHASES AND WILL RETURN TO PAY ME MY $22.95 LATER.
OR ELSE, I SHALL TRACK DOWN THE LITTLE THIEF AND STRING HIM UP BY HIS HEELS.
THANK YOU, AND HAVE A NICE DAY, SIR!

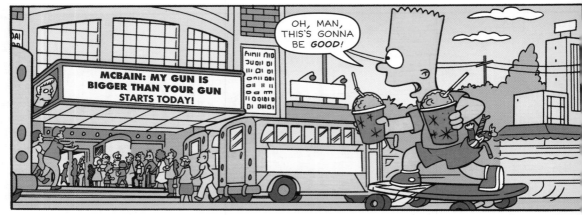

OH, MAN, THIS'S GONNA BE *GOOD!*

MCBAIN: MY GUN IS BIGGER THAN YOUR GUN STARTS TODAY!

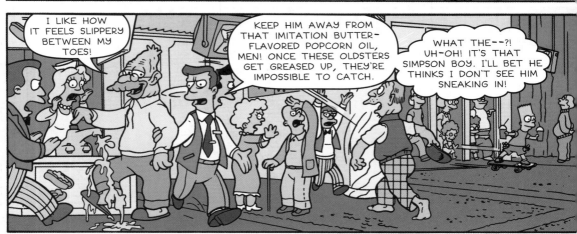

I LIKE HOW IT FEELS SLIPPERY BETWEEN MY TOES!

KEEP HIM AWAY FROM THAT IMITATION BUTTER-FLAVORED POPCORN OIL, MEN! ONCE THESE OLDSTERS GET GREASED UP, THEY'RE IMPOSSIBLE TO CATCH.

WHAT THE--?! UH-OH! IT'S THAT SIMPSON BOY. I'LL BET HE THINKS I DON'T SEE HIM SNEAKING IN!

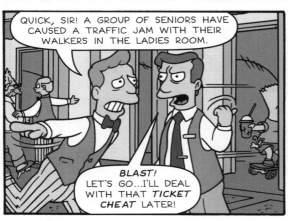

QUICK, SIR! A GROUP OF SENIORS HAVE CAUSED A TRAFFIC JAM WITH THEIR WALKERS IN THE LADIES ROOM.

BLAST! LET'S GO...I'LL DEAL WITH THAT *TICKET CHEAT* LATER!

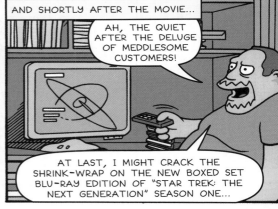

AND SHORTLY AFTER THE MOVIE...

AH, THE QUIET AFTER THE DELUGE OF MEDDLESOME CUSTOMERS!

AT LAST, I MIGHT CRACK THE SHRINK-WRAP ON THE NEW BOXED SET BLU-RAY EDITION OF "STAR TREK: THE NEXT GENERATION" SEASON ONE...

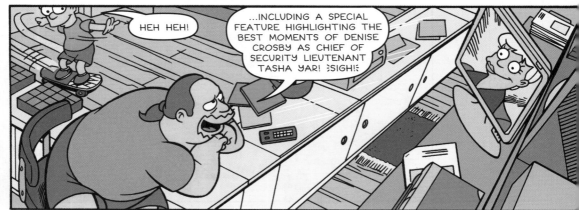

HEH HEH!

...INCLUDING A SPECIAL FEATURE HIGHLIGHTING THE BEST MOMENTS OF DENISE CROSBY AS CHIEF OF SECURITY LIEUTENANT TASHA YAR! ⸮SIGH!⸮

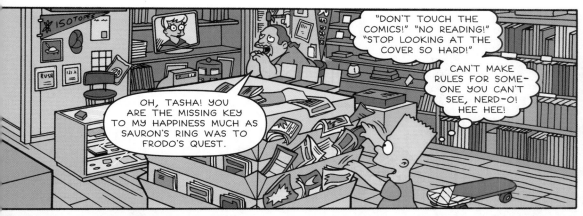

"DON'T TOUCH THE COMICS!" "NO READING!" "STOP LOOKING AT THE COVER SO HARD!"

CAN'T MAKE RULES FOR SOME- ONE YOU CAN'T SEE, NERD-O! HEE HEE!

OH, TASHA! YOU ARE THE MISSING KEY TO MY HAPPINESS MUCH AS SAURON'S RING WAS TO FRODO'S QUEST.

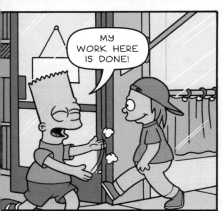

MY WORK HERE IS DONE!

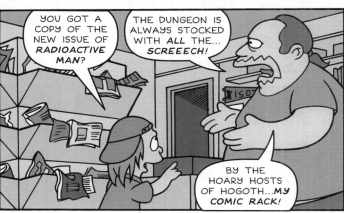

YOU GOT A COPY OF THE NEW ISSUE OF *RADIOACTIVE MAN*?

THE DUNGEON IS ALWAYS STOCKED WITH *ALL* THE... SCREEECH!

BY THE HOARY HOSTS OF HOGOTH...*MY COMIC RACK!*

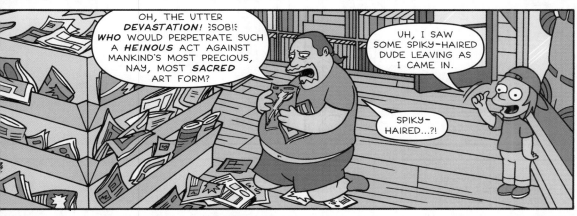

OH, THE UTTER *DEVASTATION!* ⸮SOB!⸮ *WHO* WOULD PERPETRATE SUCH A *HEINOUS* ACT AGAINST MANKIND'S MOST PRECIOUS, NAY, MOST *SACRED* ART FORM?

UH, I SAW SOME SPIKY-HAIRED DUDE LEAVING AS I CAME IN.

SPIKY- HAIRED...?!

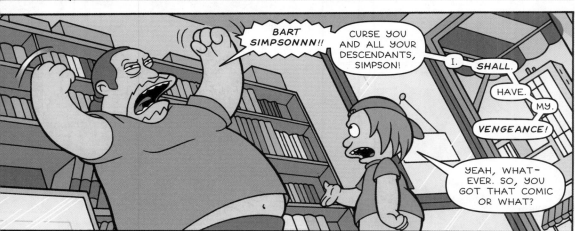

BART SIMPSONNN!!

CURSE YOU AND ALL YOUR DESCENDANTS, SIMPSON!

I. *SHALL.* HAVE. MY. *VENGEANCE!*

YEAH, WHAT- EVER. SO, YOU GOT THAT COMIC OR WHAT?

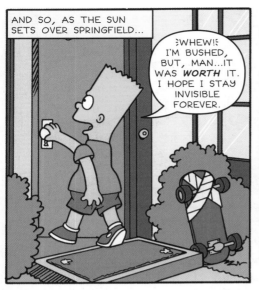

AND SO, AS THE SUN SETS OVER SPRINGFIELD...

≥WHEW!≤ I'M BUSHED, BUT, MAN...IT WAS *WORTH* IT. I HOPE I STAY INVISIBLE FOREVER.

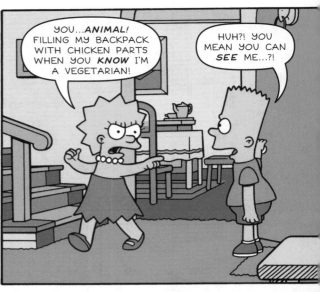

YOU...*ANIMAL!* FILLING MY BACKPACK WITH CHICKEN PARTS WHEN YOU *KNOW* I'M A VEGETARIAN!

HUH?! YOU MEAN YOU CAN *SEE* ME...?!

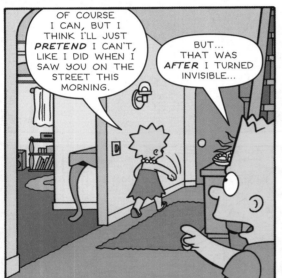

OF COURSE I CAN, BUT I THINK I'LL JUST *PRETEND* I CAN'T, LIKE I DID WHEN I SAW YOU ON THE STREET THIS MORNING.

BUT... THAT WAS *AFTER* I TURNED INVISIBLE...

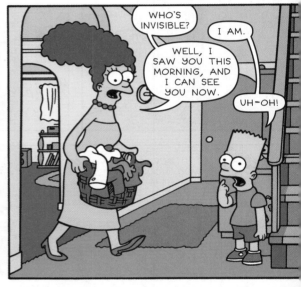

WHO'S INVISIBLE?

I AM.

WELL, I SAW YOU THIS MORNING, AND I CAN SEE YOU NOW.

UH-OH!

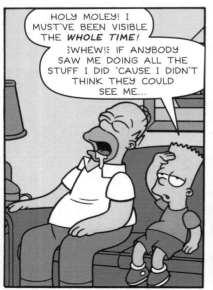

HOLY MOLEY! I MUST'VE BEEN VISIBLE THE *WHOLE TIME!* ≥WHEW!≤ IF ANYBODY SAW ME DOING ALL THE STUFF I DID 'CAUSE I DIDN'T THINK THEY COULD SEE ME...

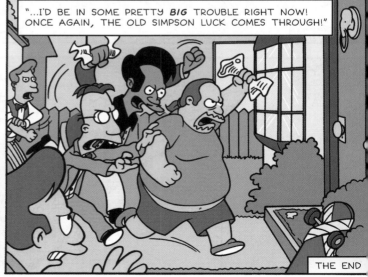

"...I'D BE IN SOME PRETTY *BIG* TROUBLE RIGHT NOW! ONCE AGAIN, THE OLD SIMPSON LUCK COMES THROUGH!"

THE END

MAGGIE'S CRIB

by ARAGONES

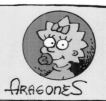

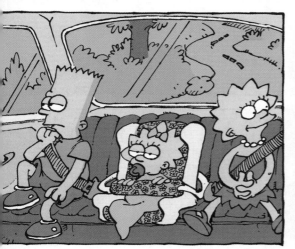

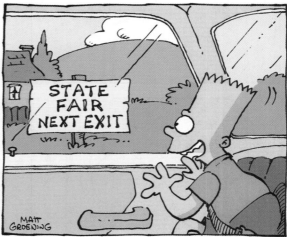

STATE
FAIR
NEXT EXIT

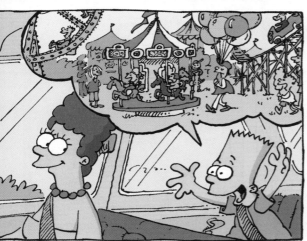

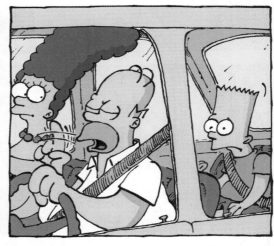

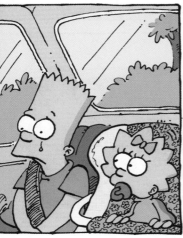

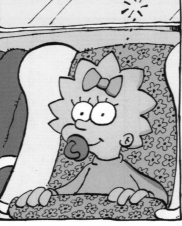

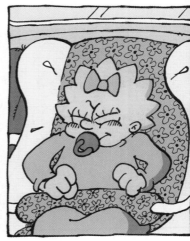

SERGIO ARAGONÉS
STORY & ART

ALAN HELLARD
COLORS

BILL MORRISON
EDITOR

STATE FAIR
RING O TOSS

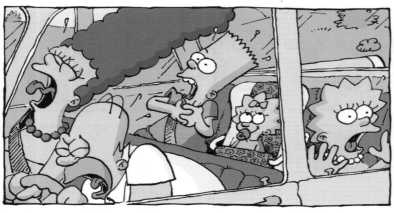

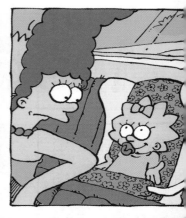

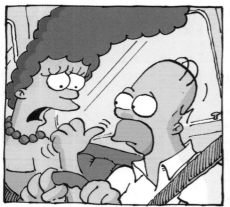

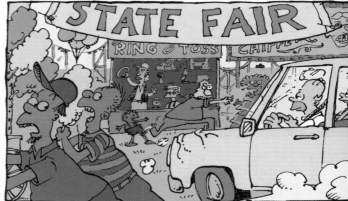

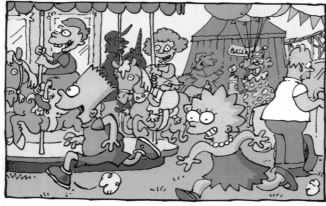

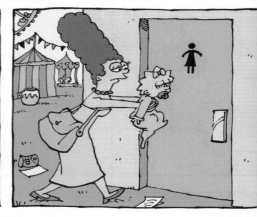

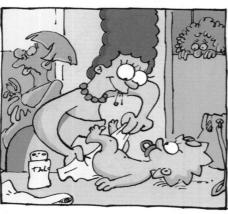

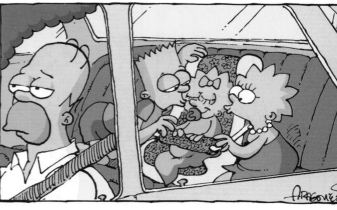

Li'L KRUSTY

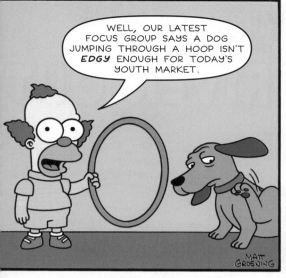

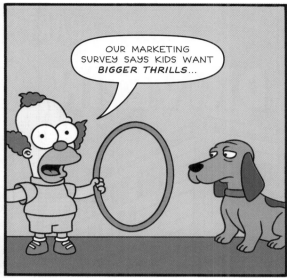

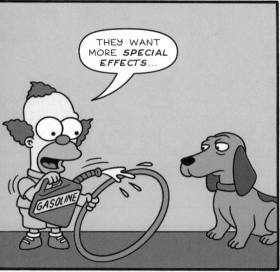

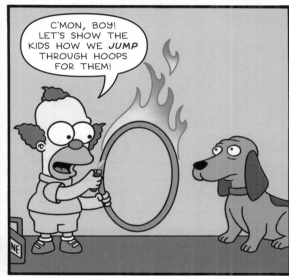

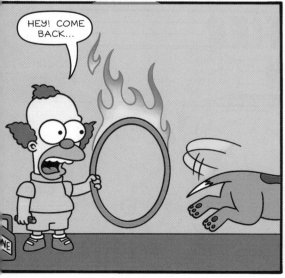

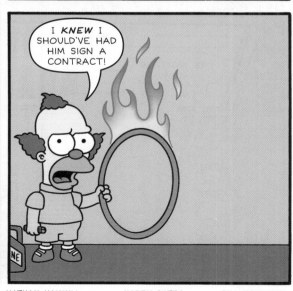

MARY TRAINOR
SCRIPT

JASON HO
PENCILS

MIKE ROTE
INKS

NATHAN HAMMILL
COLORS

KAREN BATES
LETTERS

BILL MORRISON
EDITOR

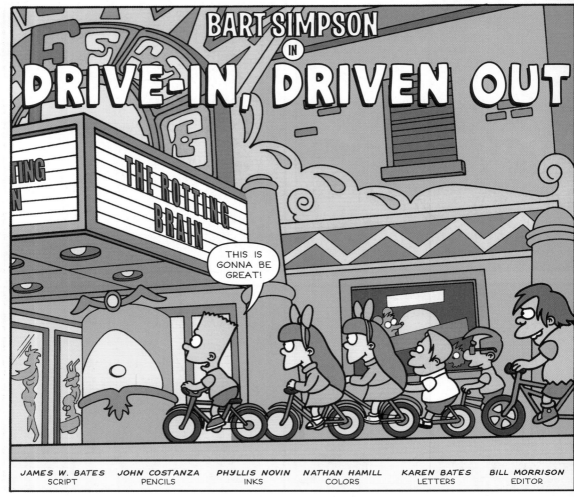

BART SIMPSON IN DRIVE-IN, DRIVEN OUT

THE ROTTING BRAIN

THIS IS GONNA BE GREAT!

JAMES W. BATES	JOHN COSTANZA	PHYLLIS NOVIN	NATHAN HAMILL	KAREN BATES	BILL MORRISON
SCRIPT	PENCILS	INKS	COLORS	LETTERS	EDITOR

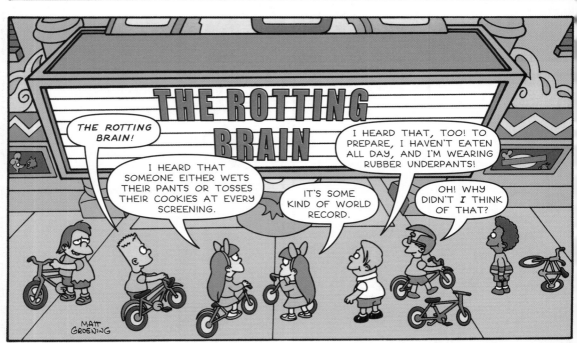

THE ROTTING BRAIN

THE ROTTING BRAIN!

I HEARD THAT SOMEONE EITHER WETS THEIR PANTS OR TOSSES THEIR COOKIES AT EVERY SCREENING.

IT'S SOME KIND OF WORLD RECORD.

I HEARD THAT, TOO! TO PREPARE, I HAVEN'T EATEN ALL DAY, AND I'M WEARING RUBBER UNDERPANTS!

OH! WHY DIDN'T *I* THINK OF THAT?

MATT GROENING

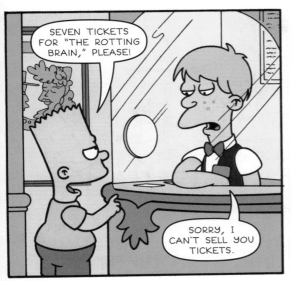

SEVEN TICKETS FOR "THE ROTTING BRAIN," PLEASE!

SORRY, I CAN'T SELL YOU TICKETS.

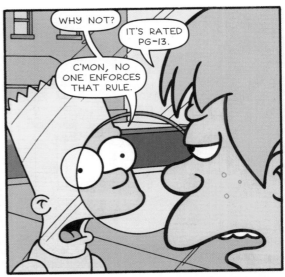

WHY NOT?

IT'S RATED PG-13.

C'MON, NO ONE ENFORCES THAT RULE.

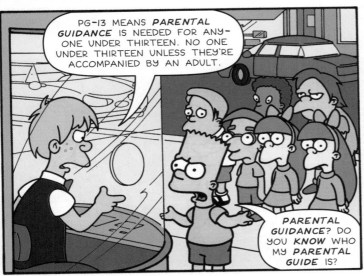

PG-13 MEANS *PARENTAL GUIDANCE* IS NEEDED FOR ANY- ONE UNDER THIRTEEN. NO ONE UNDER THIRTEEN UNLESS THEY'RE ACCOMPANIED BY AN ADULT.

PARENTAL GUIDANCE? DO YOU *KNOW* WHO MY *PARENTAL GUIDE* IS?

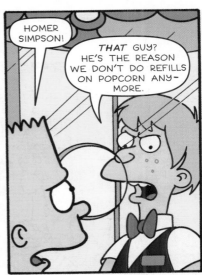

HOMER SIMPSON!

THAT GUY? HE'S THE REASON WE DON'T DO REFILLS ON POPCORN ANY- MORE.

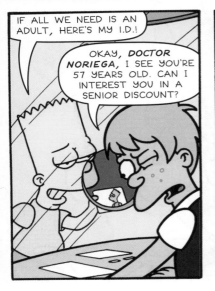

IF ALL WE NEED IS AN ADULT, HERE'S MY I.D.!

OKAY, *DOCTOR NORIEGA*, I SEE YOU'RE 57 YEARS OLD. CAN I INTEREST YOU IN A SENIOR DISCOUNT?

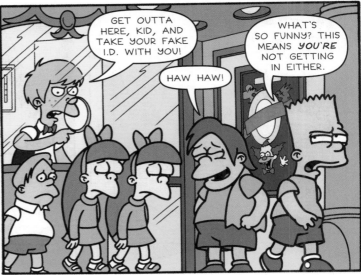

GET OUTTA HERE, KID, AND TAKE YOUR FAKE I.D. WITH YOU!

HAW HAW!

WHAT'S SO FUNNY? THIS MEANS *YOU'RE* NOT GETTING IN EITHER.

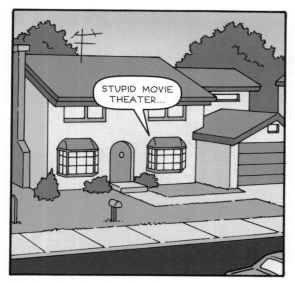

STUPID MOVIE THEATER...

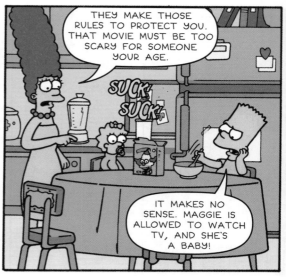

THEY MAKE THOSE RULES TO PROTECT YOU. THAT MOVIE MUST BE TOO SCARY FOR SOMEONE YOUR AGE.

SUCK SUCK!

IT MAKES NO SENSE. MAGGIE IS ALLOWED TO WATCH TV, AND SHE'S A BABY!

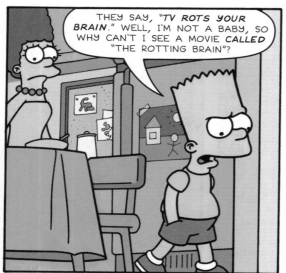

THEY SAY, "TV ROTS YOUR BRAIN." WELL, I'M NOT A BABY, SO WHY CAN'T I SEE A MOVIE CALLED "THE ROTTING BRAIN"?

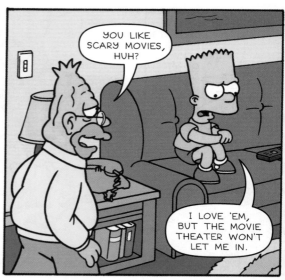

YOU LIKE SCARY MOVIES, HUH?

I LOVE 'EM, BUT THE MOVIE THEATER WON'T LET ME IN.

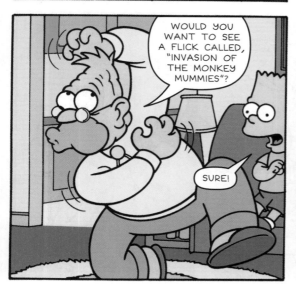

WOULD YOU WANT TO SEE A FLICK CALLED, "INVASION OF THE MONKEY MUMMIES"?

SURE!

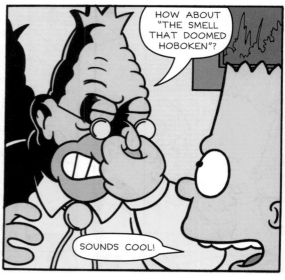

HOW ABOUT "THE SMELL THAT DOOMED HOBOKEN"?

SOUNDS COOL!

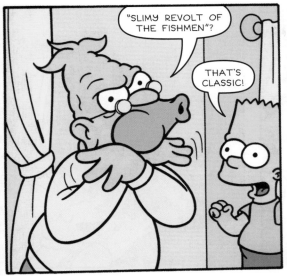

"SLIMY REVOLT OF THE FISHMEN"?

THAT'S CLASSIC!

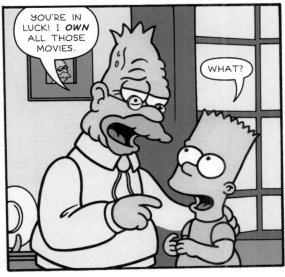

YOU'RE IN LUCK! I *OWN* ALL THOSE MOVIES.

WHAT?

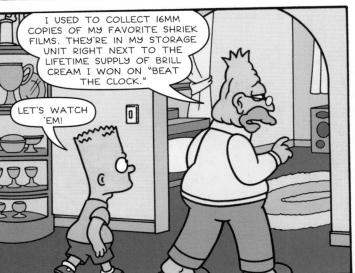

I USED TO COLLECT 16MM COPIES OF MY FAVORITE SHRIEK FILMS. THEY'RE IN MY STORAGE UNIT RIGHT NEXT TO THE LIFETIME SUPPLY OF BRILL CREAM I WON ON "BEAT THE CLOCK."

LET'S WATCH 'EM!

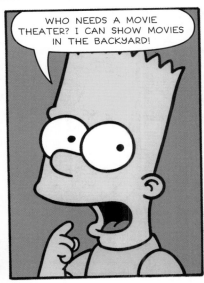

WHO NEEDS A MOVIE THEATER? I CAN SHOW MOVIES IN THE BACKYARD!

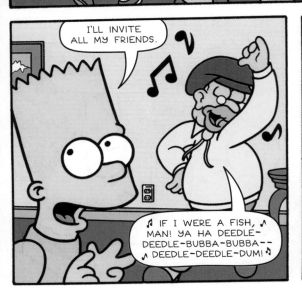

I'LL INVITE ALL MY FRIENDS.

♪ IF I WERE A FISH, ♪ MAN! YA HA DEEDLE-DEEDLE-BUBBA-BUBBA-- ♪ DEEDLE-DEEDLE-DUM! ♪

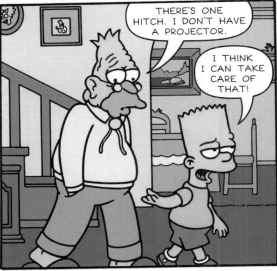

THERE'S ONE HITCH. I DON'T HAVE A PROJECTOR.

I THINK I CAN TAKE CARE OF THAT!

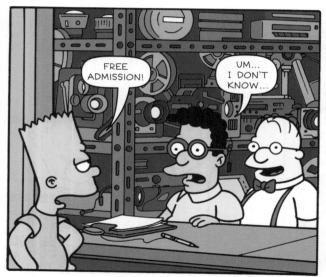

FREE ADMISSION!

UM... I DON'T KNOW...

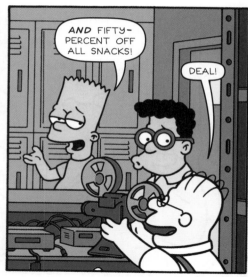

AND FIFTY-PERCENT OFF ALL SNACKS!

DEAL!

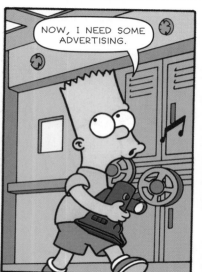

NOW, I NEED SOME ADVERTISING.

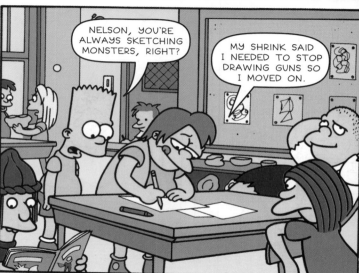

NELSON, YOU'RE ALWAYS SKETCHING MONSTERS, RIGHT?

MY SHRINK SAID I NEEDED TO STOP DRAWING GUNS SO I MOVED ON.

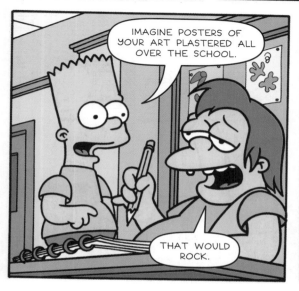

IMAGINE POSTERS OF YOUR ART PLASTERED ALL OVER THE SCHOOL.

THAT WOULD ROCK.

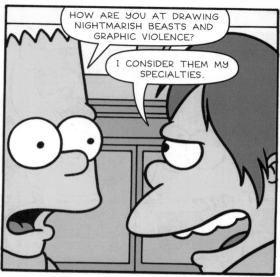

HOW ARE YOU AT DRAWING NIGHTMARISH BEASTS AND GRAPHIC VIOLENCE?

I CONSIDER THEM MY SPECIALTIES.

EXCELLENT!
BART SIMPSON'S MONSTER MOVIE DRIVE-IN
RIDE YOUR BIKE OR HIKE!
FRIDAY NIGHT
BE THERE TO BE SCARED!
A DRIVE-IN THEATRE IN YOUR BACKYARD?
IT'S MORE OF A RIDE-IN.
WHAT MOVIE ARE YOU SHOWING?
THE FIRST MOVIE IS CALLED "THE CREEPING CRUD."
EWW.
SOUNDS GROSS!
WE'LL BE THERE!
WHAT KIND OF SCAM ARE YOU RUNNING NOW?
IT'S NOT A SCAM, ***AND*** I WAS ACTUALLY THINKING THAT I NEEDED A PARTNER...
REALLY? WHAT DO I HAVE TO DO?
REMEMBER WHEN WE HAD THAT LEMONADE STAND?

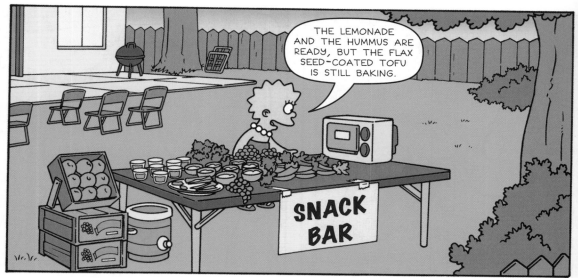

THE LEMONADE AND THE HUMMUS ARE READY, BUT THE FLAX SEED-COATED TOFU IS STILL BAKING.

SNACK BAR

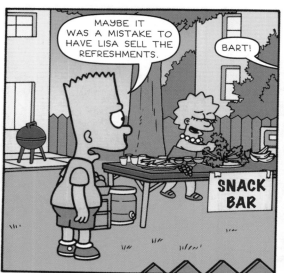

MAYBE IT WAS A MISTAKE TO HAVE LISA SELL THE REFRESHMENTS.

BART!

SNACK BAR

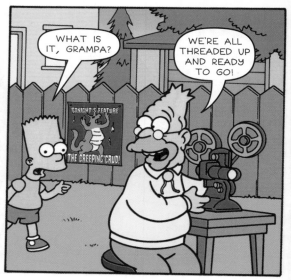

WHAT IS IT, GRAMPA?

WE'RE ALL THREADED UP AND READY TO GO!

TONIGHT'S FEATURE

THE CREEPING CRUD!

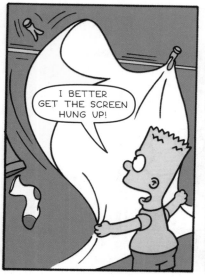

I BETTER GET THE SCREEN HUNG UP!

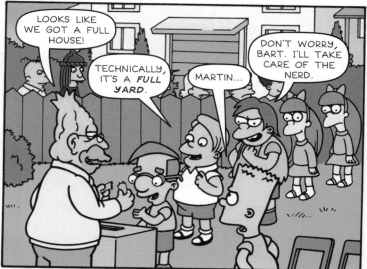

LOOKS LIKE WE GOT A FULL HOUSE!

TECHNICALLY, IT'S A FULL YARD.

MARTIN...

DON'T WORRY, BART. I'LL TAKE CARE OF THE NERD.

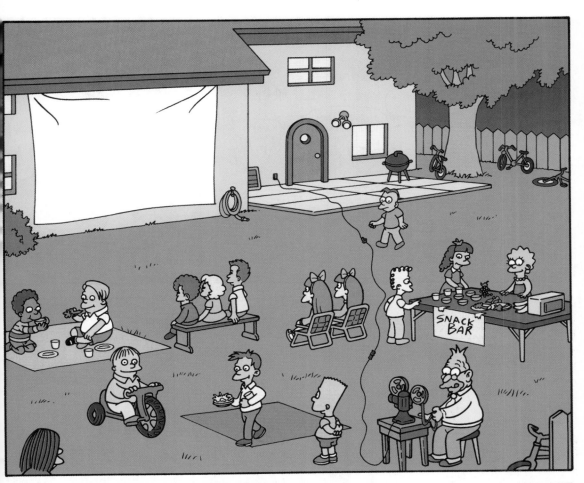

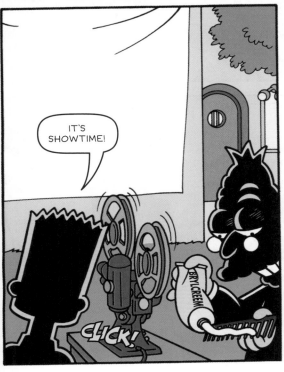

IT'S SHOWTIME!

CLICK!

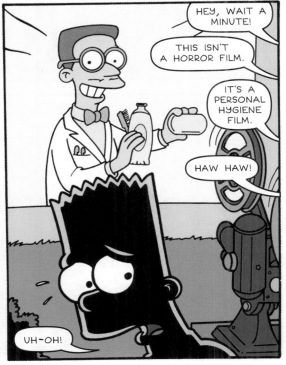

HEY, WAIT A MINUTE!

THIS ISN'T A HORROR FILM.

IT'S A PERSONAL HYGIENE FILM.

HAW HAW!

UH-OH!

THIS IS LAME!
BART'S TO BLAME!
I DEMAND A REFUND!
I WANT MY MONEY BACK, TOO!
WAIT!
SPLOP!
ICK! IS THAT HUMMUS?
NO. IT'S THE CREEPING CRUD!
STOP THROWING CELERY STALKS! I'VE GOT ANOTHER MOVIE!
NIGHT OF THE MOLE PEOPLE
GRAMPA, PLEASE TELL ME THIS ONE IS A HORROR MOVIE.
HMM...MY MEMORY IS A LITTLE SHAKY ON THIS ONE.
MILLIONS OF AMERICANS HAVE FACIAL MOLES, BUT THAT'S NO REASON TO BELITTLE THEM.
BOO!
ANOTHER HEALTH MOVIE? I DIDN'T KNOW. SERVES ME RIGHT FOR BUYING IT OVER THE INTER-WEB THINGY.
SO MUCH FOR THE BACKUP MOVIE.
I KNEW I HAD TO HAVE A PLAN B WHEN GRAMPA'S INVOLVED, BUT I SHOULD'VE HAD A PLAN C!

I GOT A COMPLAINT THAT YOUR BACKYARD MOVIE THEATRE IS MAKING TOO MUCH NOISE.
WE'RE JUST TRYING TO WATCH A MOVIE!
THEY WON'T LET US KIDS IN TO SEE HORROR MOVIES AT THE AZTEC, SO WE'RE WATCHING THEM HERE.
I HATE THE AZTEC. THEY MAKE ME PAY FOR TWO SEATS.
THE PROBLEM IS THAT ALL MY MOVIES ARE OLD HEALTH AND HYGIENE FILMS.
I LOVE THOSE! THEY'RE SUCH A HOOT.
"THE HOUSE OF EAR WAX" **AND** "THE BLOODY NOSE."
NOBODY LEAVES UNTIL THEY'VE SEEN BOTH OF THESE CLASSICS!
MY NAME IS **CRUD**.
THE END

Li'L KRUSTY

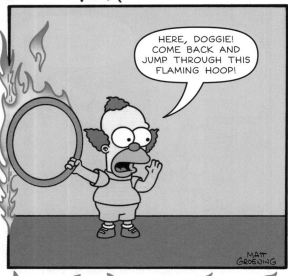

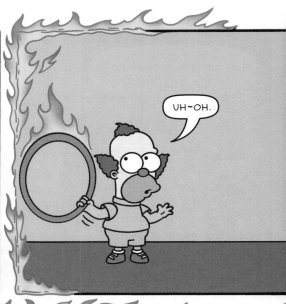

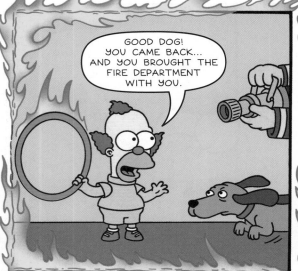

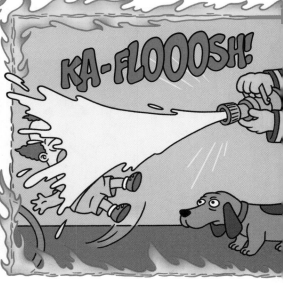

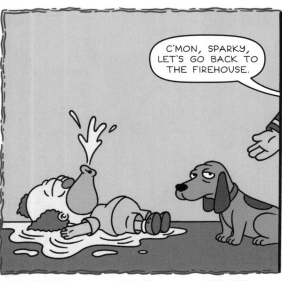

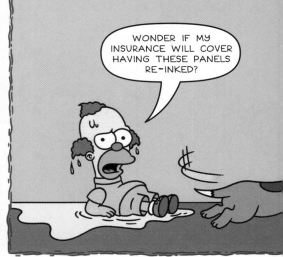

MARY TRAINOR
SCRIPT

JASON HO
PENCILS

MIKE ROTE
INKS

NATHAN HAMMILL
COLORS

KAREN BATES
LETTERS

BILL MORRISON
EDITOR

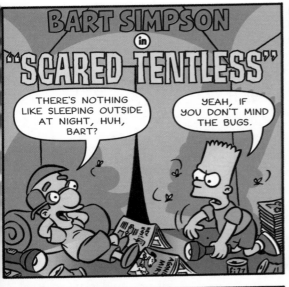

BART SIMPSON in "SCARED TENTLESS"

THERE'S NOTHING LIKE SLEEPING OUTSIDE AT NIGHT, HUH, BART?

YEAH, IF YOU DON'T MIND THE BUGS.

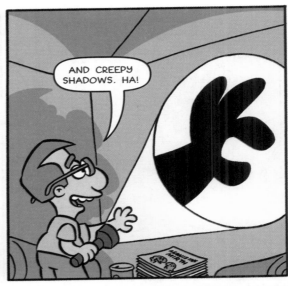

AND CREEPY SHADOWS. HA!

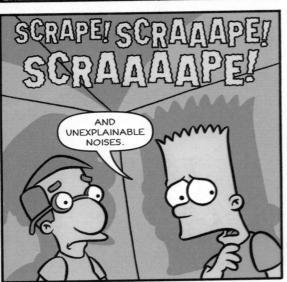

SCRAPE! SCRAAAPE! SCRAAAAPE!

AND UNEXPLAINABLE NOISES.

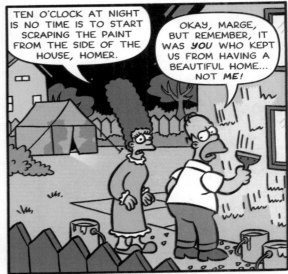

TEN O'CLOCK AT NIGHT IS NO TIME IS TO START SCRAPING THE PAINT FROM THE SIDE OF THE HOUSE, HOMER.

OKAY, MARGE, BUT REMEMBER, IT WAS *YOU* WHO KEPT US FROM HAVING A BEAUTIFUL HOME... NOT *ME*!

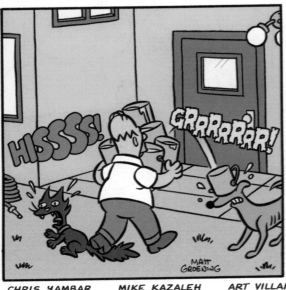

HISSSS!

GRRRRRRR!

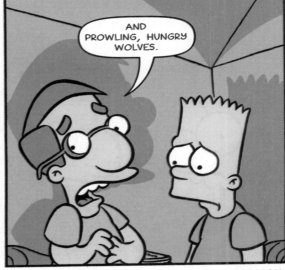

AND PROWLING, HUNGRY WOLVES.

CHRIS YAMBAR
STORY

MIKE KAZALEH
ART

ART VILLANUEVA
COLORS

KAREN BATES
LETTERS

BILL MORRISON
EDITOR

GNAWWW! SCROOMPFF! SLURPPP!
SLURPP! GNAWWRL!
AND BLOODSUCKING VAMPIRES.
WOULD YOU MIND KEEPING IT DOWN, HOMER? THE SOUND OF YOUR EATING IS ENOUGH...
...TO WAKE THE DEAD!
AND THAT ARMY OF UNDEAD ZOMBIES THAT ARE HIDING OVER THERE IN THOSE BUSHES.
AAAAAAAAAH!
WE NOW RETURN TO "NIGHT OF THE BLOODEATING GHOULS" ON ZOMBIE MATINEE.
SO HOW'S THE CAMPING GOING TONIGHT, BOYS?
JUST F-FINE, D-D-DAD.
W-WOULD YOU MIND CHANGING THE CHANNEL, MR. SIMPSON?
THE END

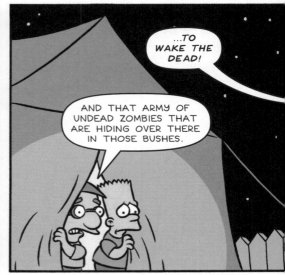

BART SIMPSON in
BIG TOP FLOP

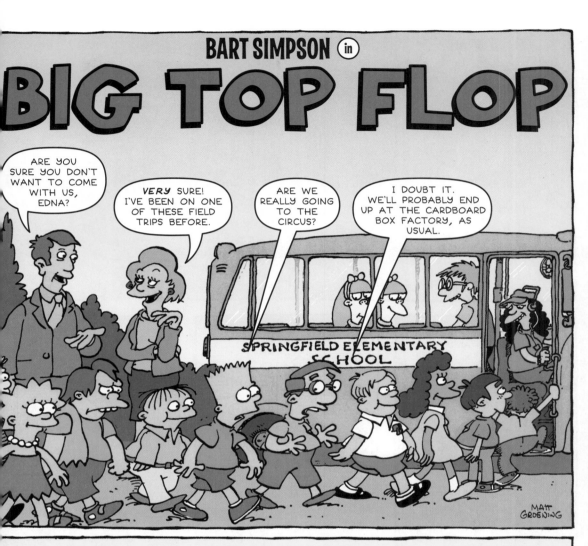

ARE YOU SURE YOU DON'T WANT TO COME WITH US, EDNA?

VERY SURE! I'VE BEEN ON ONE OF THESE FIELD TRIPS BEFORE.

ARE WE REALLY GOING TO THE CIRCUS?

I DOUBT IT. WE'LL PROBABLY END UP AT THE CARDBOARD BOX FACTORY, AS USUAL.

SPRINGFIELD ELEMENTARY SCHOOL

SERGIO ARAGONÉS
SCRIPT & ART

ART VILLANUEVA
COLORS

KAREN BATES
LETTERS

BILL MORRISON
EDITOR

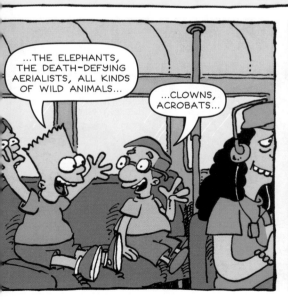

...THE ELEPHANTS, THE DEATH-DEFYING AERIALISTS, ALL KINDS OF WILD ANIMALS...

...CLOWNS, ACROBATS...

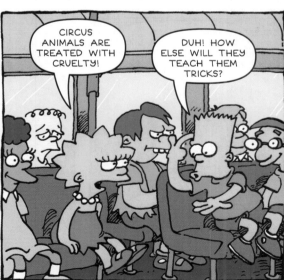

CIRCUS ANIMALS ARE TREATED WITH CRUELTY!

DUH! HOW ELSE WILL THEY TEACH THEM TRICKS?

STOP! WAIT, THERE'S THE CIRCUS, OTTO! WHERE ARE YOU GOING?
ELEMENTA
SCHOOL
THIS TIME, WE'RE GOING TO THE *CIRQUE DU LUNE!* NO ANIMALS, JUST THE ELEGANT ART OF MIME AND THE SUBTLE FANTASY OF ASIAN CONTORTIONISTS!
YEAH!
HAW HAW!
BLAH!
HEY, WAIT A MINUTE! I WANNA SEE ANIMALS, TOO!
WHERE ARE THE TIGERS WHEN YOU NEED THEM?
SPRINGF
SC

THIS BITES! I WANT TO SEE THE TIGERS!
THE ELEPHANTS!
THE SWEET SMELL OF SAWDUST AND CLOWN MAKE-UP!
TO BE SCARED!
THIS IS SCARY ENOUGH!
I GOT IT! LET'S GO TO THE REAL CIRCUS!
GREAT IDEA! BUT HOW?
BY FIRST GETTING OUT OF THIS ONE!
AH, THAT TINGLING SENSATION ONE GETS FROM ACTING IN A REGRETTABLE FASHION!
I'M WITH YOU GUYS! ANYTHING BUT MIMES!

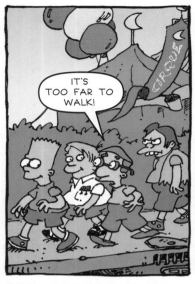

IT'S TOO FAR TO WALK!

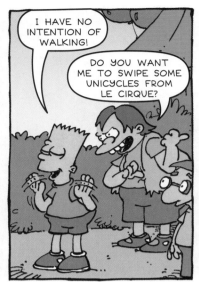

I HAVE NO INTENTION OF WALKING!

DO YOU WANT ME TO SWIPE SOME UNICYCLES FROM LE CIRQUE?

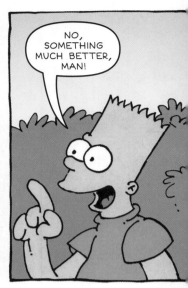

NO, SOMETHING MUCH BETTER, MAN!

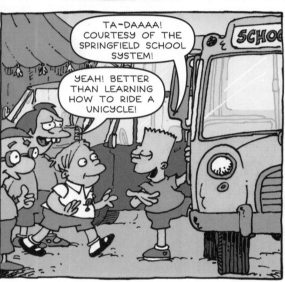

TA-DAAAA! COURTESY OF THE SPRINGFIELD SCHOOL SYSTEM!

YEAH! BETTER THAN LEARNING HOW TO RIDE A UNICYCLE!

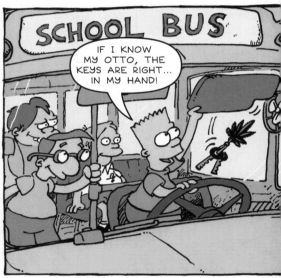

IF I KNOW MY OTTO, THE KEYS ARE RIGHT... IN MY HAND!

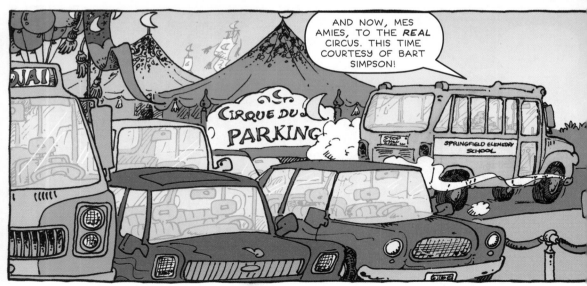

AND NOW, MES AMIES, TO THE *REAL* CIRCUS. THIS TIME COURTESY OF BART SIMPSON!

NOW THIS IS WHAT I CALL A CIRCUS!
TICKETS
UH-OH! I JUST REALIZED SOMETHING...
...WE NEED SOME MONEY!
SORRY, I GAVE MY LUNCH MONEY TO NELSON!
SO DID I!
NOTHING LEFT! I USED IT FOR LUNCH!
HAW HAW!
HEY, THAT'S MY LINE!
POW!
AH, THE SORROW OF FAILURE. GUESS IT'S BACK TO THE FLOCK FOR US!
NOT TO WORRY! WE'LL USE THE OLD "SNEAK UNDER THE TENT" TRICK!

TO BE USED ONLY WHEN MR. SECURITY GUARD ISN'T AROUND!
BUT DON'T WORRY. THERE'S OUR TICKET IN... THE CHINESE DRAGON!
NOW WE JUST WALK IN!
I KNEW IT ALL THE TIME! BART, YOU ARE PURE GENIUS!
ONCE INSIDE, WE DITCH THE DRAGON AND CHOOSE THE BEST SEATS IN THE HOUSE!
I CAN'T SEE ANYTHING!
I CAN SEE...SAND AND SAW-DUST!
WE'RE IN!
IF YOU SAY SO. I STILL CAN'T SEE ANY-THING!
NEITHER CAN I!
I'M FOLLOWING YOU GUYS! I CAN'T SEE NOTHIN' EITHER!
HEY, THERE'S THE DRAGON!
WELL... LET'S GET READY!

OW!
SLAP!
HEY, THAT HURTS!
WACK!
OUCH! I THOUGHT SPANKING WENT OUT WITH THE TWENTIETH CENTURY!
SPLATT!
OUCH!
OOOOCH!
I THOUGHT THEY DISCONTINUED THE DRAGON BIT!
THEY DID! THE GUYS INSIDE COMPLAINED TOO MUCH ABOUT THE SLAPPING!
OW! CUT THAT OUT!
WHICH IS THE FUNNY PART OF THE ACT!
I DON'T SEE ANYTHING, BUT EVERYONE IS LAUGHING!
HOW COME I'M NOT? OW!
PLEASE, BART, TAKE US OUT OF HERE!
SIMPSON, TOMORROW YOU'RE GIVING ME DOUBLE LUNCH MONEY!
I DIDN'T SEE ANYTHING BUT STARS! OUCH, MY GLUTEUS MAXIMUS!
THERE HAS TO BE A BETTER WAY!

I NEVER THOUGHT A TRIP TO THE CIRCUS COULD BE SO PAINFUL!
WAIT! I SEE THE SOLUTION NOW!
THERE!
NO WAY I'M GETTING INSIDE THE LION'S CAGE!
ME, NEITHER! NO WAY!
NO, NO...WE JUST GET INSIDE THESE THINGS AND WALK IN!
I CAN'T SEE ANYTHING!
AT LEAST IF WE GET HIT, WE WON'T FEEL ANYTHING!
THIS WAY! JUST FOLLOW THE LIGHT!
THE FLYING MORRISONS
WE'RE IN!
I CAN'T SEE! LET'S GET OUT OF THIS THING!
I CAN'T MOVE IT!! I'M TRAPPED!
I CAN'T MOVE IT, EITHER...

EVERYONE IS APPLAUDING AGAIN, AND I STILL CAN'T SEE ANYTHING!
HELP! I'M TRAPPED!
I CAN'T LIFT THIS THING!
NOW!
I'M FOLLOWING YOUR FEET!
AND I'M FOLLOWING YOURS!
I'VE HAD IT! I'M WALKING BACK TO JOIN THE OTHERS!
THIS TIME, LET'S DRIVE IN!
I DUNNO... THIS CAR IS KINDA SMALL. AND IT HAS NO SEATS!
OKAY, MOVE IT! WE ALL HAVE TO FIT INSIDE!
HOW DO YOU START THIS CAR?

HEY, THE CAR HAS CUSHIONS NOW!
THAT'S MY BUTT!
MOVE OVER! *I* ALWAYS DRIVE THE CAR!
THIS IS DISGUSTING!
OUCH! ARE WE IN?
I CAN'T SEE ANYTHING!
IT STINKS IN HERE! *YEAGH!*
I'M BEING CRUSHED!
HA HA HA HA
THAT'S MY FACE YOU'RE STEPPING ON!
WHAT'S HAPPENING? I STILL CAN'T SEE ANYTHING!
I LOST A SHOE!
OH NO! WE ARE OUTSIDE AGAIN!
WE MISSED ALL THE FUN!
MY GLASSES... HELP ME LOOK FOR MY GLASSES!

THIS TIME, WE'RE IN FOR SURE!
GET IN! THEY JUST ANNOUNCED THE NEXT ACT, AND THIS IS IT!
HURRY! THEY'RE COMING FOR THE CANNON!
THE GREAT ZAPPO
WE'RE MOVING!
ARE YOU SURE WE'LL SEE SOMETHING THIS TIME?
SURE! THIS TIME WE'LL HIT THE TARGET!
KAA-BOOM!
WAAA!
MY GLASSES!

...TWELVE, THIRTEEN...AND, OF COURSE, WE'RE MISSING THE FOUR BOYS OF THE APOCALYPSE.
WHEN I GROW UP, I WANT TO WORK IN THE CIRQUE DU LUNE!
ME, TOO!
THE MOST AMAZING THING HAPPENED! I WAS PARKED AT THIS CIRCUS, AND THE NEXT THING I KNEW, I WAS AT ANOTHER CIRCUS!
MAN, THAT'S MAGIC!
DON'T BE AN IDIOT, OTTO! BART, MILHOUSE, NELSON, AND MARTIN MUST HAVE TAKEN THE BUS TO GO TO THE OTHER CIRCUS!
WOW! I MUST HAVE BEEN TAKING A NAP!
HEY, THERE THEY ARE!
BEST FIELD TRIP EVER!
THE COLORS, THE SPECTACLE... I'LL NEVER FORGET THIS DAY!
IT WAS WONDERFUL!
MAGNIFICENT SHOW!
AW, SHUT UP!
The END

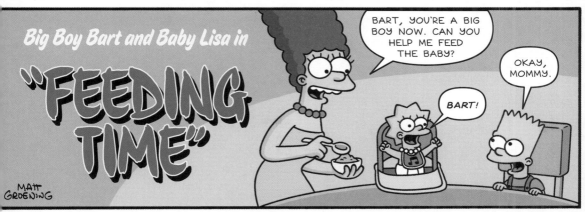

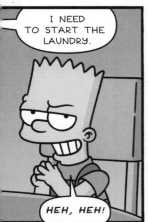

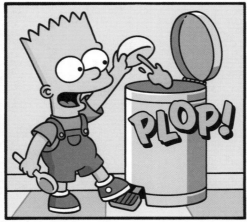

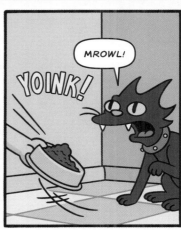

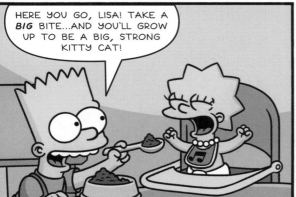

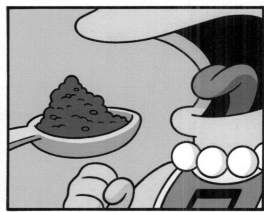

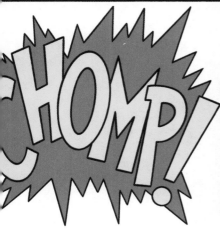

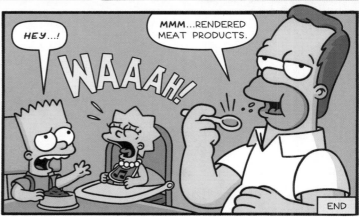

STORY BY **TERRY DELEGEANE**   PENCILS **JASON HO**   INKS **MIKE ROTE**   COLORS **ART VILLANUEVA**   LETTERS **SERBAN CRISTESCU**